TAKING HER CHANCES

When Sue inherits her auntie's run-down cottage and dog kennels in Cornwall, two very different men come into her life. There is good-looking Andy, who takes her under his wing as he works on improvements to the property. Sue feels that he would like to be more than just friends, but somehow there is no real spark between them. Then Dermot Williams moves into the farmhouse next door, and Sue is very attracted to him. But she discovers that her new neighbour is ruthless . . .

Books by Chrissie Loveday
in the Linford Romance Library:

LOVERS DON'T LIE
THE PATH TO LOVE
REMEMBER TO FORGET

SPECIAL MESSAGE TO READERS

This book is published under the auspices of

THE ULVERSCROFT FOUNDATION

(registered charity No. 264873 UK)

Established in 1972 to provide funds for research, diagnosis and treatment of eye diseases. Examples of contributions made are: —

A Children's Assessment Unit at Moorfield's Hospital, London.

•

Twin operating theatres at the Western Ophthalmic Hospital, London.

•

A Chair of Ophthalmology at the Royal Australian College of Ophthalmologists.

•

The Ulverscroft Children's Eye Unit at the Great Ormond Street Hospital For Sick Children, London.

You can help further the work of the Foundation by making a donation or leaving a legacy. Every contribution, no matter how small, is received with gratitude. Please write for details to:

THE ULVERSCROFT FOUNDATION,
The Green, Bradgate Road, Anstey,
Leicester LE7 7FU, England.
Telephone: (0116) 236 4325

In Australia write to:

THE ULVERSCROFT FOUNDATION,
c/o The Royal Australian College of Ophthalmologists,
27, Commonwealth Street, Sydney,
N.S.W. 2010.

CHRISSIE LOVEDAY

TAKING HER CHANCES

Complete and Unabridged

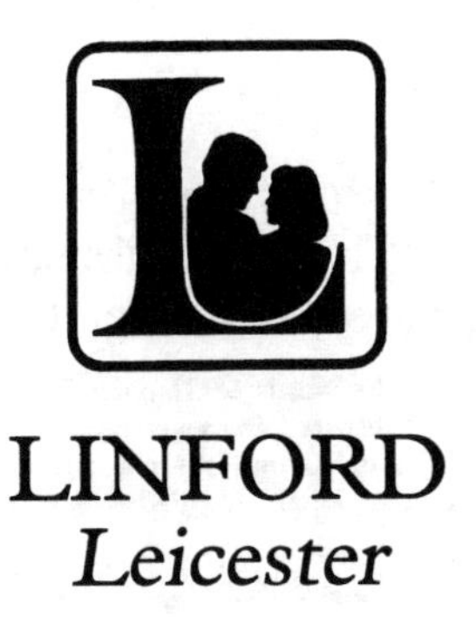

LINFORD
Leicester

First published in Great Britain

First Linford Edition
published 2002

British Library CIP Data

Loveday, Chrissie
Taking her chances.—Large print ed.—
Linford romance library
1. Love stories
2. Large type books
I. Title
823.9′14 [F]

ISBN 0–7089–9893–3

Published by
F. A. Thorpe (Publishing)
Anstey, Leicestershire

Set by Words & Graphics Ltd.
Anstey, Leicestershire
Printed and bound in Great Britain by
T. J. International Ltd., Padstow, Cornwall

This book is printed on acid-free paper

1

For goodness' sake, William,' Sue said, laughing. 'OK, I get your message,' and as she spoke, the Irish Setter burst out of the back door, tail streaming behind him and his face a perfect picture of happy excitement. 'Why can't I have that sort of energy in a morning?'

She sighed and turned back to the kitchen to put on the kettle. Once she'd had a coffee, the day might look a bit better. She wiped the sleep out of her eyes and brushed her long dark hair away from her face. A slight figure, Sue certainly did not look her twenty-five years. In her jeans and bright red T-shirt, she looked like any of the local kids who hung around the beach, just beyond the field at the back of her home.

She sat on the back step, wrapping her hands round the mug of black coffee. William rushed back to her, his eyes bright with the joy of another day and tongue flapping out of his mouth.

Fondly, Sue put her hand out to fondle the large dog. He promptly rolled over, a mass of shining fur, legs and feathery tail.

'Idiot dog,' she said. 'I suppose you think the day should have begun long ago.'

She drained her cup and dumped it back on the draining-board, along with last night's supper dishes. She refilled the kettle and put it on top of the range. It would be ready for the washing up by the time she had finished her next round of chores. One day, she promised herself, I shall have this dump re-plumbed and a proper system installed. If ever she had any spare money, it would be the first priority.

Spare money! That was a laugh. She looked over the yard to the dog kennels with their wire enclosures outside each one. Any spare money went into the animal enclosures. If she was to run a successful business, any profit so far had to be put back into improving the facilities. She began the rounds of feeding, cleaning and exercising her guests.

'Hello, Ben,' she called to the large German Shepherd.

He greeted her with a wag of the tail and strode over to the food bowl to inspect the morning rations. Sue moved to the next enclosure. She glanced at her chart and mixed the food for the little Jack Russell pup. She made a point of feeding the dogs exactly the same diet as they had at home. She even tried to keep the timing the same, as far as possible. This way, the dogs felt more secure when they were staying with her. Their owners were happier, too, certain their beloved pets were being cared for in the nearest thing possible to their normal routines.

An hour later, the first round of tasks was complete. She adored working with dogs and often found herself smiling with pure happiness. She knew how lucky she was to have a job she enjoyed so much. Sue went into the tiny office to sort out the day's mail and complete her record charts. At least the office was respectable. The cottage may be some sort of primitive hovel but the parts that clients saw were clean and bright and gave out all the right messages.

Dear old Auntie Daisy, she thought. How on earth had she managed to run this place for so long? It had come as something of a shock to inherit these run-down kennels after her aunt had died. She would never forget the day the solicitor's letter arrived. Her thoughts drifted back.

'I think Aunt Daisy must have left you something, dear,' her mother had said, handing over the large, official-looking letter to her daughter.

'Why would she do that?' Sue asked, puzzled. 'I don't even remember her. I know we visited when we went down to Cornwall for our holidays, once upon a time.'

'Maybe there was no one else,' her

mother replied with a slight tinge of sadness.

With fingers that unaccountably began to tremble, Sue tore open the envelope. The heavy vellum paper with a crest at the top made everything seem suddenly very serious. The legal language made her wonder if the words really meant what she thought they did.

'Wow! I think it means she's left me the kennels and the cottage, everything that goes with the business. Whatever am I going to do with it?'

She sat down, in a state of shock.

'I was thinking of looking for a new job. Maybe this is it!'

'Don't be ridiculous. You know nothing about running a kennels. You're a secretary, for goodness' sake. Besides, it's much too far away.'

Her mother looked suddenly scared. Her only daughter, living in Cornwall? Oh, no. It was a ridiculous idea.

'Think how William would love it down there. You know, I think I'm already warming to the idea. Why don't we all go down next weekend, just to have a look round?'

'Oh, Sue, how can you even consider the idea? Speak to your aunt's solicitors and find out what sort of state the place is in. Then you'll see what ridiculous nonsense the whole idea is.'

It wasn't the first time Sue and her mother had disagreed about what she should or should not do.

'For heaven's sake, Mum, I'm twenty-four. How many daughters of my age are still living at home? No, I think it's high time I made some sort of move. This may be exactly what I should be thinking about.'

'Most daughters of your age are usually getting married or at the very least making some attempt to settle down with a nice young man.'

'Well, obviously I'm different. I'll probably become an aged spinster, like Auntie Daisy, and live with my dogs and cats and just forget about the rest of the world.'

She was wicked to tease her mother

like this, she knew. The trouble was, her mother simply invited such behaviour.

* * *

The next few days were fraught with arguments and pleadings until finally, she left her parents with an ultimatum. Either they came with her to look at her inheritance or she was going alone. Unwillingly, Sue's mother and father packed their things into the car the following weekend and together with an over-excited Irish Setter, they set off on the long drive to Cornwall. It took most of the day to reach the little village in the far west of the county.

'I vote we book in at the pub. I doubt old Daisy's place will be fit for human habitation. I think she'd gone quite dotty after the last time we saw her and that must have been all of fifteen years ago.'

Her father was adamant and they booked into the little inn for the night.

The dog, however, was not allowed.

'You can always shut him in one of the kennels at Daisy's,' Sue's dad said with a cynical smile.

'I shall stay with him. William will go potty if he's left in a strange place for five minutes, let alone overnight. If he can't stay here, I won't either.'

She had to admit, her resolve almost failed when they saw the state of the place. Picturesque would have been a kind way to describe the cottage. A pantile roof, thick with moss, lichen and even the odd bit of grass, topped once white walls.

Great chunks of render had fallen away, leaving granite rocks exposed. Any mortar that may have kept them in place had long since vanished. The winds and rain had done the rest. Once inside the cottage, the damage showed itself in the form of patches of green mould and in some places, actual running water on the walls.

'Can we take it you will not be staying?' her father asked, after a brief glance into what must have been the sitting-room.

'I said I'd stay,' Sue said determinedly.

'Mad,' the reply came as he walked out.

He pushed the door hard and one hinge promptly broke off.

'Not even secure. For goodness' sake, Sue. You must see this is 'way beyond any chance of redemption.'

He stomped crossly down the path and sat back in the car. Sue went outside to the kennel area. Whatever state the house may have fallen into, the kennels looked clean, well kept. The wire surrounding the individual runs was relatively new.

'I could always put a mattress in one of the kennels,' Sue said brightly to her mother.

'That's about the only place you could stay,' she replied wryly. 'Be reasonable, darling. Come to the pub with us. This place is awful. William can stay in the car, just for the night. Give him a long walk in the wood and he'll be fine.'

'Oh, Mum, when will you stop treating me like a five-year-old? I'm a big girl now.'

Sue's thoughts returned to the present. All that had taken place nearly a year ago. Since then, she'd made the move, despite all the objections from her parents. And so much had happened since then. As she thought of her father, tears came into her eyes. It must be almost six months since he had died, all so suddenly. Sometimes, she realised she hadn't thought about him for almost the whole day, and felt guilty. How her mother must miss him, miss her, too. The phone rang and she pulled herself back to reality.

'Saunders' Kennels,' she said. 'Can I help you?'

'Sue? It's Andy. Dad's got a load of tiles left over from a job. You can have them cheap. Interested?'

'Floor, wall or roof?' she asked. 'And how cheap?'

'Oh, wall tiles, grey ones, and, they will not cost much at all. Tell you what, I can even come over and help you fix them. Now I can't say fairer than that, can I?'

'Excellent. We could tile the food preparation area at the side of the office. Make it look much more hygienic.'

'Sorry, no can do. These are for your pathetic excuse of a bathroom. This is the trouble with you. Everything is for the kennels. You are living in absolute squalor and your precious dogs have luxury all the way.'

'Well, it's the dogs who earn my living for me. I have to have everything looking good or the clients won't leave their beloved animals with me in the first place.'

They chatted for a while longer and agreed that Andy would come over later in the day and begin fixing tiles round the shower. In return, she promised to cook supper for the two of them. Efficiently, she dealt with the morning mail and entered a few bookings on the rather elderly computer. It may not have all the up-to-date features but it did the job and was an old friend from her office days.

She whistled for William and collected Ben from his kennel and set off on the first walk of the day. It took up a large part of her day to exercise all the dogs. William accompanied each walk and so was very fit. His eyes shone with pleasure as they went over the field to the beach. Another week or two and the annual dog ban on the beach would begin. She wanted to make the most of the glorious stretch of sand while she could.

To one side of her property, there were open fields. On the other side was a rather derelict farmhouse. Today, however, there was obviously something going on. A couple of large cars were parked outside and a builder's truck. Someone must be about to do the place up. It might be nice to have neighbours, she thought, though it could also bring some disadvantages. Living next door to a boarding kennels was hardly peaceful.

She wondered if Andy would know what was going on. Dear Andy, she thought fondly. He had really taken her under his wing. His father ran a small building company in the village and had been very helpful in getting the cottage at least marginally habitable, before she had moved in.

Andy had helped her far beyond what she could have afforded to pay. Any leftover materials from his other jobs found their way to the cottage. Half a can of paint had covered one of the bedroom walls; a second-hand electric shower unit had provided her with the means to keep herself clean; when someone in the village was having a new kitchen installed, Andy had rescued the old cupboards and put them up in her own little kitchen.

It had been a fortunate day, the day she had called in the firm to begin repairs on the damaged walls, but, apart from all his kindness, Andy was proving himself to be a good friend. She knew instinctively that he would like to be more than friends but she was not ready for that. Somehow, she had difficulty thinking of him as anything more than a brother. He was good-looking, too, tall and broad-shouldered. He enjoyed sport and was an excellent surfer. His brown hair was bleached blond at the tips and his eyes were particularly bright.

She often wondered why he was willing to spend so much time with her. After all, he could have his pick of the girls who hung around the beach. There was always a collection of them in their skimpy shorts and tight T-shirts, hoping to be noticed by the boys. But Andy never had time for any of them. Always, as soon as he finished his surfing, it was to Sue he returned. She really could do a lot worse, she thought. But somehow, there was no real spark of magic between them.

She turned and called in the dogs.

They bounded to her and she set off back home and to the rest of her guests. The smaller dogs, she took into the field behind the kennels and threw balls for them to chase. There were two Jack Russells and a couple of mongrels who all played well together.

They exercised each other to some extent, saving her a lot of time and energy. A quick hose down for each kennel and her main chores were over for the morning.

It's not such a bad life, she thought. Fresh air and exercise, glorious surroundings and time spent with her beloved dogs. Even if there was very little money, she was happy and enjoyed the freedom of being her own boss. This was where she wanted to be for the next few years, if not for ever.

2

Sue was still giving her charges their evening feed when Andy arrived. He gave her a wave and indicated the boxes of tiles as he went inside the house. She finished her chores and went into the cottage. Andy had already unpacked several of the tiles and was busy drawing lines on the wall.

'Phew. You don't let the grass grow under your feet, do you?' she said with a laugh.

'If I don't make a start, a job never gets done,' he replied, smiling. 'Had a good day?'

'Fine thanks. You?'

He nodded.

'Oh, did you know someone is doing up the farm next door? There were people there most of the day. Maybe your dad could get some work.'

'I doubt it. They've got some high-powered London architect involved. No doubt they'll bring the workers down, too. Nothing so lowly as us locals. The owner's something to do with computers. They reckon he's made a fortune and is retiring down here.'

Andy's voice held an unusually cynical note, for him. He and his father were both very hard workers but were never likely to make huge amounts of money. Not if they treated everyone the way they did her, she thought. Even if she could have afforded it, Andy put in many more hours work than he was ever paid for.

'Shame. Be nice if you could get a slice of some rich cake. Talking of food, I'd better get something organised for supper. What do you fancy?'

'Isn't it more a case of what there is?' he said with a wry grin.

However good her intentions, Sue's domesticity left something to be desired.

'We could always go down to The

Fisherman's. I'll treat us to something.'

'You're very sweet, Andy. You're already doing far too much for me. No, I can rustle up something to eat. I may not be Cornwall's answer to Delia Smith, but I cook a mean chilli. That do you?'

He nodded, gripping a pencil between his teeth as he worked on the tiling. She watched him as he began to place the tiles, each one in perfect symmetry with its neighbour. If it had been up to her, they'd be slipping all over the place.

He was undoubtedly everything a girl could want. Why then, did she only feel affection and not heart-stopping love for the man? She turned and went back into the kitchen. She began to wash the pile of dishes from the morning. Somehow, she never did seem to get round to such simple chores until forced by necessity.

By eight o'clock, Andy and Sue were sitting at the little kitchen table, finishing two generous plates of chilli and rice.

'That really hit the mark,' he said appreciatively. 'Thank heavens you're not one of those women who picks at their food. I can't stand it when you take someone out for a meal and all they do is nibble at a lettuce leaf.'

She laughed.

'I was never known for my ability to diet. I'm lucky, I guess. One of those rare folk who doesn't put on weight. Coffee now?'

'How about a walk with William? He keeps looking at me in that way of his that suggests I'm keeping you away from him. I'm beginning to feel quite guilty.'

'Take no notice. He's perfected that look. You simply have to ignore it.'

The setter lifted his head, somehow knowing the conversation was about him. He thumped the ground with his long tail and panted, looking every bit as if he was laughing.

'How does that great long tongue ever fit back in his mouth?' Andy asked.

William thumped the ground with his tail.

'OK,' Sue said, 'we'll do what you suggested and have coffee when we get back. You win, dog, as usual.'

She pushed her chair away from the table as the telephone rang.

'It's OK. The answering machine's on. I can call whoever it is later.'

When she heard the strange voice cut in with the answering machine, Sue froze. They were almost out through the door, when she heard the message.

'Miss Saunders? Could you please call urgently. It's about your mother. The number is . . . '

That was as far as the man got, before Sue dashed back in and snatched up the receiver.

'Hello. Yes, I'm here.'

'Miss Saunders? It's Doctor Heath. I'm afraid your mother is unwell.'

'What's wrong with her? Has she had an accident? Is she all right?'

'She seems to have had some sort of stroke. She's fully conscious but rather muddled. She has agreed to go to hospital. I'm going to take her in now, for a check-over. Just a precaution. I do think it would be helpful if you could visit, however. She may need a good deal of nursing care for some while. We shall be able to assess the long-term situation in a few days.'

'I see. Just how bad is she really, Doctor?'

'She's very confused. She can't be left on her own. She'll be in hospital for a day or two at least. I imagine you will need a bit of time to make any arrangements.'

For the next few minutes, Sue listened, asked questions and noted down all the details. By the time she had hung up, she found herself shaking and gratefully accepting the mug of coffee from Andy. As soon as he had realised what was happening, he'd put on the kettle, turned William out for a run in the garden and stacked the dirty dishes in the sink.

'Thanks, you're very kind. Oh,

heavens, poor Mum. What ever am I going to do? Ben's due to stay here for another week and there are already several other bookings for next week.'

'We'll sort something out. Isn't there anyone you can call on to help?'

Andy looked concerned. The boarding-kennel was purely a one-man business. The profits were non-existent so far and Sue was only just beginning to turn it round.

'I hardly know many people at all. There's no way I could afford to take on extra help, yet. What a mess. But I have to go to Mum. If I could somehow leave things ticking over here for a few days. I can assess the situation after that.'

'I'll do anything I can to help. I could exercise the dogs in the evenings and do the evening feeds, if you can sort someone out to do the morning rounds. Or maybe I should take some time off.'

They discussed various ideas, Sue grateful for Andy's kindness. As he left her at the end of the evening, he put a gentle arm round her shoulders and kissed her forehead. She felt tears pricking the back of her eyes.

'Don't be afraid to ask. Anything we can do to help. You're very special to me, Sue,' he said.

'Andy, thank you so much. You've been great. I'll call you in the morning.'

He hesitated, as if there was something more he wanted to say but thought better of it. He strode off down the path and she heard his van start up and he drove away. She called her dog and together, they made the final rounds of the kennels. The wind was blowing and she could smell the tang of the sea in the night air.

'Oh, Wills, I hope we don't have to leave this place. I love it so much.'

The dog sensed her mood and licked her bare leg comfortingly.

She slept fitfully. However concerned she was about her mother, the immediate practicalities of looking after the dogs in her care filled her mind. If only she had been able to train someone else to follow the routine she had established. But she could think of no one who might help.

At seven the next morning, the phone rang again. Her heart pounding, she rushed to answer it. Anyone calling this early must have bad news. It had to be about her mother.

'Hello?' she whispered.

'Are you OK?' came the comforting voice of Andy. 'You sound dreadful.'

'Sorry. Yes, I'm fine.'

'Right, I think I've come up with something. Mum says she'll come and feed the dogs in the mornings, if you can show her what to do. I'll come in around four and clean out and exercise the dogs.'

'That's really good of you, but there's an awful lot to do in the mornings. It would be too much to ask of your mum.'

'The dogs will just have to wait to be cleaned out till the afternoon. The weather's set fair, for a few days at least. The dogs can spend most of their time in the runs. Don't worry. At least it will keep things going until you know what's to happen. Actually, thinking about it, it might make sense if I stayed there, just while you're away. Yes, that's the answer. Don't worry about a thing. I'll be over in half an hour and we'll get everything organised. Dad will have to manage without me for a while.'

Before she could protest or say another word, Andy put the phone down. It seemed he was about to organise her thoroughly. It was really rather nice. Andy was so reliable and kind. She would never be able to thank him enough.

* * *

A few hours later, she was driving the last few miles back to her old home. It was her first visit there since she'd stayed following her father's death. Already, she began to dread the very idea of returning to the safe life she had once known. Cornwall had gripped her totally in its unique magic. She loved the open views, the peaceful countryside and above all, the joy of working in her own kennels. How could she possibly return to her old home and work in an office again?

The house was silent and dark when Sue stopped her car. She let herself in and shivered. It seemed remote to her, like entering a stranger's house. The life she had once known there had gone. Tears sprang to her eyes as memories flooded back. She swallowed hard and picked up the phone to dial the hospital. Her mother was recovering well, though much of her ability to communicate had been impaired by the stroke.

'She'll probably soon be back to her old self,' the nurse assured her. 'You can come and see her anytime you like.'

Sue crossed her fingers. Somehow, she sensed that everything was about to change. Even if her mother did recover sufficiently, how could she be left on her own? Life could never be the same again. She quickly made a call to Andy to let him know she had arrived and to make sure all was well at her beloved kennels. Then with a lump in her throat, she set out for the hospital.

If her mother was ever to get back to her old self, Sue realised she would have to make a dramatic improvement. The frail woman lying in a hospital bed seemed as far removed from her mother as anyone could be. Sue gulped, shocked at the sudden change in her. She knew it was selfish but all she saw was her life crashing in ruins around her. Her recent thoughts about Andy, and the future, flew right out of the window. There could be no possible future for her with Andy, or anyone else for that matter.

'Hello, have you come to visit me?' her mother said.

'Hello, Mum. How are you feeling?'

'Mum? Are you my mother, dear?' she asked her daughter, and Sue stared.

'You are my mum,' she said quickly. 'Don't you recognise me?'

The occupant of the bed shook her head in bewilderment.

'I've come up from Cornwall to visit you.'

'That's nice of you dear. My husband should be here soon. Perhaps he will give you a lift home. Do I know you?'

With tears filling her eyes and a lump in her throat, Sue took her mother's hand. She held it tightly and rested her head against the back of the chair. Her mother seemed to fall asleep and gently, Sue pulled her hand away. She got up from the chair quietly and went to look for a doctor. She needed someone to tell her how to deal with all of this. She was filled with the sense of losing both of her parents. It was too cruel.

It seemed like hours later before she was driving back to her old home. She felt bone weary, no longer able even to think clearly. She was in no state to come to terms with everything the doctor had said. She let herself into the silent house and made a milk drink.

She had eaten next to nothing all day and the long drive had taken its toll. She felt weak and slightly dizzy. She found some biscuits and nibbled one or two with her drink. It was too late to eat properly now and probably the best thing she could do would be to go to bed.

Another week in hospital for her mother and then full-time nursing care, the doctor had said. How on earth was she to manage that? She slumped down on the large, comfortable sofa in the living-room. It was an old friend from her childhood. It had been a boat, or a camp or any number of other things in her imagination. It felt warm, cosy and familiar. She wished for a moment, that she was still small and could get totally lost in one of her imaginary worlds. She closed her eyes and despite her teeming brain, she slept heavily for several hours.

When she awoke, she felt stiff and heavy-eyed. It was around four o'clock in the morning. She felt totally alone and miserable, and wished like crazy that she had not left her beloved William behind. Andy had persuaded her that the trip would be easier without him. He was right, of course, but she longed for the dog's warming presence and enthusiasm for life. Undemanding, unconditional love was what he offered.

Wide-awake now, Sue went into the kitchen and looked for something to eat. She cooked some bacon and eggs and made a pot of coffee. Her mother had always kept a good supply of food in the fridge and freezer. Once she had eaten, she felt more calm and her mind began to sift through the various possibilities.

If she remained here in Hertfordshire, she would have to find some sort of work. That would still mean she would have to leave her mother for long periods during the day. If, on the other hand, her mother were to move to Cornwall, once she was strong enough, Sue would be able to keep her kennels.

She could probably run the business, as well as being on hand to see to things for her mother. It was really the only way.

Then she thought of the tumble-down, little cottage in Nancetowan and her heart sank. How on earth could her mother live there? Only a couple of the rooms were even remotely habitable. There was no hot water on tap and the whole place needed re-wiring. She would be facing bills of thousands of pounds. Her bank balance was virtually nil.

On the other hand, she thought, as she looked around, if her mother was to move to live with her, she would no longer need this house. If only she could be persuaded to sell up, everything could be solved. But it would all take time and that was the one thing they did not have. But it looked like the only sensible solution. Her mother had few ties with her old life since Sue's father had died.

Once fired with her plan, Sue could

scarcely wait to set things moving. Her first call was to Andy. She knew he was an early riser and would be busy doing the first chores soon after seven. He was filled with enthusiasm. He promised to help with the essential work on the cottage and sounded delighted to learn that she would be returning soon.

After she had finished speaking, she realised that once again, he was making plans for her, for them. In the middle of everything else, she was aware of nagging doubts. She felt as if she was being sucked into a deeper relationship by the man's kindness. The more things he did to help, the harder it would be to refuse him in the end, always assuming she were to refuse him. He had not actually said anything yet, along the lines of romance. Instinctively, she knew that he would, sooner or later. She would have to face that when and if it happened.

For now, there were many more pressing problems. In another hour, she would have to face returning to the hospital. She still had to decide how she would tackle her mother about her idea for moving them both to Cornwall. It was not going to be easy.

3

Hello, Mum, how are you feeling today?' Sue asked as she took the chair beside her mother's bed.

'Sue? Is that really you?' the frail-sounding voice said.

Sue felt tears pricking her eyes. Her mother had recognised her this morning, actually known who she was. After the previous evening's visit, it was such a relief. She took the pale, limp hand and pressed it to her mouth.

'Mum,' she whispered, 'it's so good to see you.'

'And you, too, dear. When can I come home? I don't like the tea they make here. I tried to tell them the right way to make it, the way I like it. But there's never anyone to listen.'

'You'll just have to make do with the tea here, for a while.'

Sue laughed. Whatever had been

wrong with her mother, it now seemed she was very much on the mend. Things were going to be all right, after all. She was on the verge of promising to see about her mother's discharge from hospital when she was interrupted.

'I have a daughter you know,' her mother said.

The voice was less firm and seemed dreamy and far away.

'She's got some sort of business, animals, pets. Oh, dear, what are they called? Dogs, I think it is. Yes, dogs. Though what anyone wants to keep a dog for, I shall never know. Always liked cats myself. What about you, dear? Have you come to give me my physiotherapy?'

'It's Sue, Mum. Your daughter. The one who keeps dogs.'

'Oh, no, she's in . . . somewhere. I forget the place. You can't be the doctor. You're much too young.'

As quickly as Sue's hopes had risen, they were dashed once more. Clearly, her mother was going to be confused for some time, for ever, perhaps. The doctor was not too hopeful last night. Periods of lucidity followed by a total lack of recognition, he had said. Her words would be often confused or lost altogether. Her intention of talking with her mum about any plans for the future was now impossible. Time was such a pressure, though. She had to get back to her work. Andy could not be expected to cope for more than a few days.

'Is it lunch time yet?' her mother asked.

'It's a bit early for lunch. Maybe someone will bring you a cup of coffee soon,' Sue managed to say.

She felt as if her whole world was crashing round her. That short burst of normality from her mother had come and gone so quickly. Now, she would have to see the doctor again and try to talk about her plans.

'I'll be back soon. I have to go and see someone,' she said.

'All right dear. I'll wait here till you get back and then we can go shopping together. You'd like that, wouldn't you, dear?'

'That'll be fine, Mum. See you in a few minutes.'

She rose quickly and almost ran towards the door. She must see the doctor again. How on earth was she going to cope?

Half an hour later, Sue was sitting on a seat outside the hospital. Her mind was racing once more, planning, sifting the options. The doctor seemed to think that Sue's mother would need to stay in the hospital for another week. After this, virtually full-time care would be needed. Yes, there were nursing homes, but it would be expensive for anything more than a short stay. After all, Mrs Saunders was a relatively young woman still.

However much she tried to consider it, Sue knew her own decision was already made. Was she being selfish, wanting her mother to move to

Cornwall? Was is so wrong of her to want to get back to her beloved, little business? She may not have lived in Cornwall for very long, but the place had totally captivated her. She knew that she could never contemplate living anywhere else. She closed her eyes, seeing the unique blueness of the ocean that she could see from her cottage windows. She could see the towering cliffs, where waves crashed, flinging their spray high into the air.

She imagined the golden beaches with their granite, rocky bases. How William loved to chase the waves, barking madly as he played in the water as it rolled on to the beach. When Andy surfed the waves, William would leap around his board, as if he were trying to dislodge the man.

She smiled, remembering the many happy afternoons they had spent on the beach. She simply had to go back. She knew it would make little difference where her mother lived out the rest of her life. The doctor said she would most likely remain confused, though hopefully, less so than at present. At least in Cornwall, Sue could continue to earn some sort of living and release enough time to care for her mother.

She went back into the ward. Mrs Saunders was sitting up in her bed, talking to anyone who was listening, even when nobody was near.

'You're going to come and live with me in Cornwall, Mum. You'll like that, won't you? Lots of sea air. Walks on the beach.'

Sue bit her lip, uncertain if her mother was even taking anything into her poor, confused brain.

'I'm not sure your father will like it. Too far from his golf course.'

It seemed pointless to try and explain. Sue gathered up her bag and leaned over to kiss her mother.

'I'll see you later, Mum. I have to go now and get a few things sorted out. 'Bye for now.'

She placed a kiss on her mother's forehead. She must try to get things moving before her decision wavered. She managed to get an appointment to see her mother's solicitors. The solid comfort of the elderly man who had become a family friend over the years did little to calm her. It appeared that there was nothing she could do to implement her plan, at least until the legal process had been gone through.

There was nothing in place, like a power of attorney. Even if her mother was judged to be incompetent, it would take several weeks. Once that was completed, Sue would be able to organise the sale of the house and the settling of various affairs but it could take months. She bit her lip and frantically thought through the choices.

'I'll do what I can to help, my dear,' Mr Read said kindly. 'Perhaps I can put you in touch with a friend of mine. He might be able to organise a loan for you, against the property, you understand. At least then, you will be able to go ahead with some of the alterations to your house, if that's what you think is best.'

Sue nodded.

'I never dreamed it would be so complicated,' she murmured.

'It's all there to protect someone, your mother in this case. She has to agree to everything before you can proceed.'

'My poor mother couldn't even agree about what time tea is,' she said, trying not to break down. 'I only want to do what is best for her.'

'Of course you do, Sue. I know that but unfortunately, there are many unscrupulous people around who may never have their parents' best interests at heart. I'll call my friend right away and explain the situation. We'll do our best to organise something for you.'

After a very hectic day, Sue made one last visit to the hospital. She had to try and talk to her mother about some of the things she had arranged. It was evidently a rather futile gesture, but she felt she needed the chance to explain, if she could. Her mother was asleep and it seemed a pity to wake her. Sue turned and walked away. Maybe one day there would be time for explanations.

Practically dropping with fatigue, she decided against driving home that evening. She spent another night in a deep sleep, on the old sofa. When she awoke at five o'clock the next day, Sue decided it was a good time to set off on her journey back to Cornwall. She would miss the worst of the traffic in the London area and with luck, could be home by lunch-time. A quick look round her parents' house and she left. She would probably see it just once more, when she came to collect her mother. Many months ago, she had already said her goodbyes to the old place, her old life.

By eleven-thirty, Sue was pulling up in her own yard. She could hear the excited barks before she had even switched off the engine. A mad bundle of red-brown fur hurled itself at the side of her car and William's huge head pushed in at her side window.

'Hello, boy,' she called, laughing. 'Did you miss me, then? Let me get out, will you?'

The big dog pranced around, his tongue lolloping out of his mouth. His expression clearly showed how delighted he was to have his beloved mistress back. She hugged him to her, a solid, comforting warmth. He wriggled away, still leaping around and barking with joy as Andy came out of the kennel building.

'No doubting who was in the yard,' he said with a grin. 'You must have been up at the crack of dawn. It's good to see you.'

'Good to be back. Nothing like an enthusiastic dog to make you forget your worries.'

'How's your mother?'

'Oh, Andy, it was so awful to see her like that. She was nothing like Mum. She barely recognised me. She kept talking about my father, as if he was still alive.'

Tears welled up once more.

'Sorry,' she managed to mumble. 'I seem to have become a proper water works, lately.'

She turned to go inside the house, embarrassed by her show of emotion.

'Come here a minute,' Andy said softly.

He put his arms round her comfortingly, holding her tightly.

'I'm here for you, whenever you need me. Now, come on in and see what I've been busy doing. I'll put on the kettle, shall I? Then we're going back to our place. Mum's got lunch ready for us all.'

Sue allowed herself to be led. It was so nice to have someone strong to rely on, for however short a time. She gazed at her little kitchen, her jaw dropping in amazement.

'Goodness, you've done so much in just a couple of days. You can't have slept at all. It's brilliant.'

The walls had been plastered and painted and new tiles put up in all the gaps between the old cupboards and work-tops. The doors had been stripped down and revarnished. Even the floor looked better.

The old quarry tiles had been re-set in the places where they had been crumbling. They were spotless and had obviously benefited from a great deal of scrubbing.

'Mum and Dad both came over, the two evenings you were away. Mum brought the meals round and concentrated on all the cleaning and stripping of the wood. Dad and I worked on the rest.'

'How can I ever repay you all? It's wonderful. I'm so grateful. It's like taking part in one of those TV programmes, where they call in experts and fix everything.'

'Maybe we should set up in business. Change your home and your lives. What do you think?' Andy teased.

'I think the water in that kettle is ready to be poured into mugs of coffee. You're all amazing, you and your family,' Sue replied.

Andy stood smiling. His clear blue eyes glowed with a brilliance she had never noticed before. She felt bathed in their light, washed all over with something, she was unsure exactly what. He handed her a mug of coffee, his fingers lingering for a second as they touched hers. Neither of them spoke for a few moments until he broke the silence.

'There's even more. Go and look at your bathroom.'

Sue stared.

'You can't have finished the tiling there, as well. Surely not?'

He smiled and nodded towards the stair. She ran up and opened the door. The last time she had seen it, there had been tiles all over the floor in heaps, bits of rubble, plaster and off-cuts everywhere. Now, the little room was neat and tidy with beautifully-set tiles surrounding the sink and shower. The walls had been painted a brilliant yellow, contrasting with the pale blue and white patterns of the tiles. The battered old bath had been replaced and the room had space for desperately needed cupboards or drawers.

'Oh, Andy, it's wonderful. I can't believe it. How ever did you do so much?'

'Our present to you. A belated welcome to the village, if you like.'

'I'm overwhelmed,' she stammered. 'I've never known such kindness. I promise. I'll pay you back, one day. It may be a long wait, but I promise, I shall do it.'

'I said it was our gift. Now don't insult us by offering to pay, Sue. We were glad to do it. We don't want to lose you and reckoned that if things were made nicer here, you'd be more likely to stay.'

She reached out to him and put her arms round his neck and hugged him. He responded with enthusiasm. She felt his breath quicken and she hesitated slightly. She must not let him get the wrong idea but she was truly so very grateful. It meant her long-term plans seemed more attainable. With time spent decorating and refurbishing a couple more rooms upstairs, it was possible that her mother would be able to move in, much sooner than she had expected.

An hour later, they were sitting at the table of his parents' cottage nearby. They had finished a delicious meal and Sue already felt better than she had for several days.

'I don't think I shall ever be able to stop thanking you for everything you've done,' she said for the umpteenth time.

'We're pleased to have helped,' Andy's mother said, generously. 'Besides, we all know how Andy feels about you.'

'Mum,' Andy growled crossly. 'Excuse her, Sue. You know what mums are like, always trying to push you in ways they think you should go, even though you may not want to go yourself.'

Sue's smile wavered. It wasn't the

implication of Mrs Thurrock's words that stopped her. Suddenly, she felt old. Suddenly, the full truth hit her. She had reached the stage when she really did know what was best, both for herself and for her own mother.

The generation gap had come full circle and it was a sobering thought. It was something she never expected, not when her mother was relatively young. Parents always thought they knew best. Now things had changed and her mother needed her own daughter in charge.

'I really must get going. There's so much to be done. Andy, Mrs Thurrock, thank you again for everything. Please ask Mr Thurrock to let me have a bill for the materials, at the very least.'

'Don't think about it love. All left-overs from one job or another. And why not call me Alice? Less formal, don't you think?'

With still more thanks on her lips, Sue left the wonderfully-warm family that had done so much for her. There was, perhaps, the slightest trace of a frown on her face as she walked back to her own cottage. Obviously, Andy had made it plain to his parents exactly what he hoped from their liaison. He was such a lovely man — kind, generous, hard-working and very good looking.

Why then, did she feel this awful doubt? Why did she feel the need to discourage him all the time? Maybe she didn't feel the mysterious magic she had always expected when she found the right man. She liked him well enough but that elusive something was missing. She would have to proceed with extreme caution.

'I've got way too much to think about, William,' she confided in her dog a little later.

4

The following month whizzed by. Sue had to make a couple of trips back to Hertfordshire. The first was to find a suitable nursing home for her mother and the second to move her in, once she was deemed fit enough to leave hospital. She was to stay there for a month or so, until she could be moved down to Cornwall. Over the weeks, she had recovered considerably. She was still rather confused but at least she was fully mobile again. Sometimes, she was forgetful of the simplest words, reminding her daughter that the way ahead was far from simple.

During her second visit, Sue had managed to discuss her plans for both their futures. Her mother was surprisingly willing to move to Cornwall, though Sue did wonder if she really did understand all the implications. Sue breathed a sigh of relief. The burden of paying for the nursing home was now removed. Once the sale of the house had gone through, she could move some of her mother's furniture and treasured possessions down to the cottage. When the money was finally released, she could pay off the loan and make her mother's room at the cottage so much more comfortable.

'So you see, Andy, I shall soon be able to pay you properly for all the work you've done,' she said one morning.

Andy had got into the habit of calling in at the kennels on his way to work each day. He said he wanted to be sure everything was in order and that Sue was managing.

'You don't have to do this,' she had said a number of times, but Andy smiled and continued his visits.

'I like to see you and William,' he told her. 'And you don't have to pay anything. I've told you enough times. I'm glad to help out and the materials are always stuff we have lying around.'

'I find it hard to believe you are so bad at estimating what you'll need for a job, but, thanks anyway. Now, I'd better get these dogs sorted out. I've got two new ones coming in later today.'

'You seem to be getting quite well-known. I'm glad. Who knows, the business could even start to make a profit before much longer.'

Andy grinned as he got back into his van.

'See you later maybe? I'm surfing after work but I'll be round at sevenish, if that's OK. Thought we might go to the pub for a meal tonight. What do you think?'

'OK, thanks. But it's definitely my turn to pay tonight.'

He shook his head, as he drove away. Sue went into the kennel block and began her chores. She had almost a full house. The back of the building had a storeroom and she began to imagine it with an extension. It should be relatively easy. It was still early in the season and soon, loads more holiday makers would be arriving in Cornwall.

Many of the beaches had dog bans during the summer. Sad, but necessary, she had to agree. Consequently, people arrived with their pets and then had to find somewhere to leave them. She had left leaflets in many of the campsites and hotels and had gained a lot of extra business the previous summer. People needed somewhere to leave their dogs during the days, while they went out. Yes, she must definitely speak to Andy about more kennels and runs, smaller ones for the day guests.

The dogs had begun to whine when they saw her and Sue had to forget her plans for the present, while she prepared all the meals. She had become very efficient at the task and only minutes later, there was the contented sound of dogs snuffling their bowls. She opened all the doors to the sleeping quarters to allow the dogs to go out into the paved runs outside. Each dog had its own area, separated by block walls, so that there was no chance of fights breaking out among them.

Once they were outside, Sue hosed down each kennel. She put the dog bowls through the ancient dishwasher, ensuring they were absolutely clean and sterilised. She must avoid any chance of cross infections. She often smiled at the thought of the kitchen sink where her own dishes usually resided. No such luxury as a dishwasher for her but the dogs, well that was different.

She became aware of a sudden spate of barking from some of the larger dogs, including William. She went into the yard to see who was there. A large, expensive sports coupé was parked and a tall, dark-haired man was hammering on the cottage door. Wiping her hands on her overall, Sue went towards him. He was thirty-ish, she estimated, and what a looker! He was gorgeous, film-star material at the very least.

'Hi, can I help?' she called.

'I'd like to see the owner of this establishment,' he said a trifle brusquely.

'That's me. I'm Sue Saunders. Do you have a dog to board? I'm afraid I'm fully booked at present, but in a day or two . . . '

'I certainly do not have a dog. Aren't you rather young to be in charge of this place?'

Before Sue could protest about her age or anything else, William came charging round from the back of the kennel building, where he had been investigating a particularly smelly hole. Tail and ears streaming, he leaped at the stranger with great delight. A new person for him to make friends with. In horror, Sue saw the huge, muddy paw marks plaster the man's elegantly-cut grey trousers. His light blue shirt, undeniably silk, was also a victim of the setter's enthusiasm.

'Gosh, I'm sorry. William, heel,' she called sternly.

The dog, unused to her sounding angry with him, cowered down on the ground. His dark brown eyes stared up at her beseechingly, as if to say, I never meant any harm.

'Ill-disciplined beast,' the man snapped.

'He doesn't usually behave like that. He must like you. I'm sorry. I'll pay for your clothes to be cleaned,' she promised. 'Just send me the bill.'

'Oh, I will, don't doubt it.'

'Sorry, again. Now, was there something I can help you with?'

'I came to introduce myself, actually. Not much of a beginning for neighbours.'

'Oh, crumbs. You're not the man from next door?'

She was about to say that she hadn't expected him to be this young but managed to bite back her words. Someone with such a reputation of wealth should have been middle-aged at least. Sue didn't even know his name. The building work had been going on for weeks now but so far, no one in the village knew anything about him. He was obviously very rich, judging by the amount and quality of materials delivered to the place. The huge, heavy machines that were currently moving earth by the ton, to make a garden, did not come cheap.

'Dermot Williams. I'm hoping to move in fairly soon. The work is nearing completion and I shall be ready to set up my office in the next week or two.'

'I'm pleased to meet you,' Sue said, holding out her hand.

Dermot took one look at the dirty hand and hesitated before taking it.

'Sorry,' Sue said again. 'I was in the middle of hosing down the kennels.'

Suddenly she laughed. There she was, wearing scruffy green overalls and huge wellies, while her visitor looked dressed for a business meeting, apart from having mud all over his trousers and shirt! They talked for a while, inconsequential chat about Cornwall and living in a village. She talked of her previous life and job in Hertfordshire. She even found herself talking about her mother and the plans to move her down. She realised she had probably been talking too much and for too long. Sue suddenly felt embarrassed.

'Sorry. I do go on, don't I?'

The man smiled at her, not looking at all disturbed by her chat.

She continued, 'Perhaps you might like to come and have a drink one evening, when you've settled in.'

His eyebrows flicked slightly. Sue knew exactly what he was thinking. The idea of having drinks with a scruffy kid was undoubtedly the last thing on his mind. She pushed a few stray wisps of hair back into the rubber band that contained some of her mop of hair. Both of them were quite amazed to hear him agreeing to a drink. He looked surprised himself and at once Sue blushed at her ridiculous suggestion.

'Good,' she managed to stammer. 'I'll give you a call when you've moved in and had a chance to settle. What's your number or do you have one yet?'

He took out a slim leather wallet and extracted a card.

'This has my mobile number, too. I

shall look forward to meeting you again. Only please, do try to keep that dog under control. I'm not used to wearing overalls whenever I visit.'

With a grin, he turned and went back to his car. Sue watched, fascinated, as he manoeuvred the large car out of her tiny yard. She glanced down at the card between her grubby fingers.

Computer Services, she read. Could be handy when my little machine breaks down, she mused.

'OK, Wills, you're off the hook, for now.'

The setter leaped up gladly and stood with his great paws resting on her shoulders.

'Idiot dog,' she said, pushing him down. 'You did not make a good start with our new neighbour.'

Despite his rather off-hand manner, Sue couldn't help liking what she had seen of him. His apparent bad temper had been quite justified. After all, he had been well and truly leaped upon by William. The clothes he had been wearing must have cost a heap of money. In the circumstances, a display of temper of any sort was well justified. She would definitely have to phone him, if only to offer to pay for his dry-cleaning. Hopefully once the cottage had a room where she could actually entertain someone, she might repeat her invitation for drinks. Mr Dermot Williams and her kitchen did not really seem compatible. She picked up the hosepipe and returned to her chores.

When Andy called in later that afternoon, she couldn't wait to tell him about her visitor. The entire village were speculating about the newcomer and all the things that had been done to the old farmhouse.

'Don't know what you're so excited about. He's just some wealthy bloke from up-country. Couldn't even spend his ill-gotten gains locally. Everything has to come from London. If it isn't expensive, it obviously isn't worth having, in his book.'

It was not like Andy to be so aggressive, especially about someone he hadn't even met.

'You'd have loved the mess William made of his clothes then,' Sue said, trying to lighten Andy's mood. 'Only snag is, I had to promise to foot the dry-cleaning bills. Bet he won't forget, either.'

'You shouldn't have bothered. He was trespassing, wasn't he? Can't blame the dog for attacking.'

'Come on, you old grouch. William has never attacked anyone in his whole life. Just loves everyone to death.'

At last Andy's face broke into a smile. He's like the sun breaking out from behind a cloud, Sue thought in surprise. This was not usually her style of thinking, at all.

'Right, I'm off to the beach. I'll pick you up in a couple of hours,' he said as he got back into his van.

She watched him drive away. Compared to Dermot, Andy might have come from a different race. He was solid, reliable and so very kind. Dermot, on the other hand, seemed sophisticated, smart and obviously very well-off. He was also used to having his own way. In fact, she sensed he disliked anything that may get in his way.

He'd had quite an effect on her, one way or another. Ridiculous. Why, he'd even doubted that she was old enough to own her own property. The effect she was feeling must be because he was someone new coming into her life. How could she even think of liking someone, just because they were rich? She hated herself for even thinking about the man. Compared to Andy, well, he just didn't compare with Andy.

'Come on, Wills,' she called. 'Let's go and see what's happening down at the beach.'

The dog ran to her, enthusiastic as always. She stuffed a lead in her pocket, just in case she needed it. He would never leave her side when they were walking. Sometimes, there were a great many children around and she worried that they might be scared of the large dog. Not that he would hurt a soul, of course, but the summer ban on dogs on the beaches had begun. She'd probably need to restrain him, once he caught sight of the waves.

The usual crowd of youngsters was hanging around the little lifeguard station. Several of the boys were posing against their surf-boards, casually eyeing the talent around. A group of giggling girls, none of them more than fifteen or so, was perched on the sea wall. They were all fully aware of the boys' glances and played up to them. It was part of the game, Sue smiled to herself, as she overheard their chatter.

'There's that Andy Thurrock,' one girl said. 'Now there's a hunk, if you like that sort of thing.'

'Don't be daft,' another one called. 'He's virtually an old man. Besides, everyone knows he's got the hots for that new kennel woman.'

From the corner of her eye, Sue saw them nudging each other and pointing at her. She coloured slightly, trying to stifle her own laughter. So, everyone knew that Andy had the hots for her, did they? She only suspected it but if everyone knew, well, there must be something to it!

She turned away from the little gathering and strode off to climb the steep cliff path. She felt good. She was fit and healthy. The sun was just beginning to fall lower in the sky, reflecting great gold streamers in the sea. It was cooler than during the day, when she had already walked miles to exercise all the dogs in her care. Naturally, William had taken part in every one of the walks but he still had boundless energy for more.

At the top of the cliff, she could see over the whole bay. It always gave her a thrill to view the expanse of land, fringed as it was by banks of pink thrift at this time of year. She could see Andy far below, dressed in his black wet-suit and riding his luminous yellow board. He stood still, waiting for the next big wave to break. He watched and skilfully leaped on his board with perfect timing. He rose to his feet and leaned first one way, then the next, riding the wave until he finally reached the sand.

Some of the people watching, down on the beach, gave him a round of applause. No doubt about it, he was very good. He turned with an easy grace and paddled his board out for the next wave. William peered over the top with keen interest. He didn't understand why his mistress wouldn't let him go on the beach. He would have loved to crash into the waves, barking and trying to chase them.

'Come on, William, let's go,' Sue said.

Back home, she showered and changed into clean jeans and a check shirt. She brushed her hair and tied it back with a scarf. She pulled a face in her mirror. Maybe she did look too young. Maybe it was time to try something new. Her hair perhaps? She could get it cut. She might try wearing skirts occasionally, instead of always living in trousers. She heard a car stop and barks from several dogs, and ran down the stairs to meet Andy. He was standing leaning on his van. His hair was still damp from his shower and curled softly into his neck. He grinned as she came towards him.

'Was that you I saw up on the cliffs?'

'No dogs allowed on the beach, so you were allowed to surf without William's help for once. Don't think he was too pleased. You did well. Some spectacular waves.'

'It's the championships soon. I've set my heart on winning the cup this year, before I get too old for such things.'

Sue laughed. She repeated some of the comments she had overheard from the girls. She omitted the one about him having the hots for her.

'Right. Shall we get on our way? Where do you fancy? Lobster Pot or Fisherman's?'

'Don't mind either. You choose. Better make the most of my freedom.

Mum will be here in a couple of weeks. No more evenings out for a while.'

Andy stared at her. He had never given it a thought. Obviously, she would not be able to leave a sick old lady in a house by herself. The arrival of Mrs Saunders was about to change all their lives, to some extent or another.

5

'Your Mr whatever-his-name-is certainly has made his mark on the old farm. Have you seen it lately?' Andy asked as they drove home.

'I can hardly miss it. And he's not my Mr-anything. Williams, actually.'

'No wonder you like him. Same name as your dog. Well, nearly.'

'I didn't particularly like him. I was just interested to meet him,' she protested.

The morning's encounter had cropped up more than once in the conversation during the evening.

'I only said he might help update my computer. Well, people like him probably throw out things that are much newer than my battered old thing.'

'What do you need a new one for? You're not even interested in something fantastic like the Internet. You should think about it. Right, there we are. Am I going to be invited for a coffee tonight?'

' 'Course you are, silly. Thanks for this evening. It's been great.'

Sue got out of the van and opened her door. William bounded out of the house, delighted to see both of them.

'I'll put the kettle on,' she called.

The answering machine was flashing and she pressed the play button, as she always did as soon as she was home. It was a habit she had begun recently, since her mother was taken ill.

'Hello? Sue? It's Dermot. Thought I'd give you a call to say that I have to go back to London in a couple of days. If we are to have that drink you suggested, we ought to fit it in tomorrow, if you're free, of course. Please call me back.'

'And what drink was that?' Andy asked.

His blue eyes seemed to be flashing with something close to anger, Sue thought.

'Oh, I was just trying to be

neighbourly, trying to make up for the dog mud that was ruining his trousers and shirt. Nothing special.'

'He's a bit pushy, isn't he?' Andy snapped.

'Not really. I told you, I asked him to come round for a drink sometime. It's no big deal. I'm free to invite my friends, aren't I?'

He hesitated for a moment and then spoke again.

'Sorry, I am being an oaf. Of course you must see your friends, if that's what this character is. I just didn't want to waste an evening. Like you said, we may not have the freedom to go out whenever we want to in the future.'

'You're welcome to come, too, if you want.'

'Wouldn't dream of intruding,' he said with an almost convincing grin.

'I'd better go and do my last rounds,' Sue said with a yawn.

'I'll come with you. Make sure you are all right.'

He was very protective, she thought,

almost too protective. Maybe that's what was wrong between them. She felt a little stifled by him. She was not used to having someone making so much fuss of her.

'There, all safely tucked up in their beds,' Andy teased as they came out of the kennel building. 'Got the padlock?'

He fixed it to the door and snapped it shut.

'Thanks,' Sue said. 'Thanks again for tonight. I must go to bed now, I can hardly keep awake.'

'Good-night, Sue. Sweet dreams.'

He put a hand on her shoulder and leaned over to kiss her on the cheek. He hesitated and then put an arm round her slim shoulders and drew her towards him. Very gently, he kissed her lips. She felt herself responding but always holding back, just a little. The peck on her cheek had felt almost brotherly. The other kiss served only to confuse her even more. Why could she feel nothing more than brotherly love for this apparently perfectly man?

Sue was up early as usual the next morning. As well as her day's work, she hoped to have time to clean the house a little. She also needed to go out and buy something to offer her guest that evening. Her finances did not run to keeping anything in the way of drinks in the house. Somehow, instant coffee or economy tea bags did not seem like Mr Dermot Williams' style. She would have to buy a halfway decent bottle of wine, at the very least.

She glanced at her watch. By the time Andy had left last night, she thought it had been too late to call her neighbour. Nine o'clock. Dermot must be up by now. He'd probably had builders crashing round for hours. She pulled his card from her pocket and punched the numbers into her phone.

'Dermot,' she said to his answering machine, 'thanks for your call. You are welcome to come over for a drink this evening. I'm afraid the place isn't up to much yet, so don't have any high expectations. Around seven, if that's

OK. Look forward to seeing you. Oh, and don't forget to bring your drycleaning bill. I'll keep William under control, I promise.'

The last words were drowned by a loud bleep as his machine cut out. She pulled a face, thinking she must make sure she did actually have some cash in the house. It meant a trip into Redruth to go to the bank.

'Ah, well, Wills, we have to make sacrifices sometimes. You already cost me a fortune in food so I don't suppose cleaning someone's trousers will even show up on your account.'

She worked quickly and was soon ready to make her trip into the little town. She changed into clean jeans and set off. She picked a bottle of wine from the selection at the small supermarket, hoping that Dermot wasn't too great a connoisseur. It wasn't the cheapest but certainly not the most expensive. She added some savoury nibbles to her basket and a few basics that she might need over the next few days.

She disliked shopping and could hardly wait to get back home. As she drove through the flower-bordered lanes, she wondered how anyone could bear to live in towns. She had always assumed she would live in London, once she left home. Now, she resented every minute she spent away from her little cottage.

After lunch, she took the first batch of dogs into the large field beside her own land. They ran and leaped after balls, barking and playing like noisy children. The field was leased to her on a very small annual rent. It was a godsend to her when she had so many dogs staying, as they were able to exercise without long walks. Though she loved walking, Sue simply did not have enough hours in the day for the one-person business. This way, they were given plenty of freedom and exercise. In fact, she suspected that many of them got more attention from her than their owners and often went home fitter than when they came.

She put them all back in their kennels and went to make some attempt at cleaning the cottage. The kitchen was bright and cheery and once she had cleared away all the dishes and thrown out the rubbish, it was even welcoming. The sitting-room was an utter mess and no way could be used for entertaining. Whenever Andy came round, they always perched on kitchen stools. The sitting-room was the next job on her list.

Once her mother was living here, there would be loads of furniture so Sue had simply postponed the whole thing. Once the walls were replastered, she would paint the room and then think about making it nice. The kitchen was the only option for entertaining Dermot. He was only a casual acquaintance after all. The whole invitation had been no more than a gesture of goodwill.

It was almost seven o'clock before Sue went upstairs to change. She took a very quick shower and was pulling on an almost clean pair of cream trousers, when she heard a car stop. Hair still damp, she flung on a shirt and brushed through her hair with her fingers, as she ran down the stairs. Grabbing William's collar, she opened the door. Dermot stood on her doorstep with a huge bunch of flowers and a bottle of champagne.

'Come in,' she said, slightly breathless. 'What lovely flowers. You shouldn't have.'

'Nonsense,' he said, bringing a waft of expensive aftershave with him. 'And this is to make amends for my bad temper the other day.'

'You were quite justified.' She smiled. 'Go to your basket William,' she commanded in a stern voice.

The setter gave her the sort of glare that spoke volumes. He looked accusingly at her as he sat down heavily, every movement showing exactly what he thought of the idea.

'He's a remarkable animal,' Dermot said with a grin. 'I've never had much to do with dogs before.'

Sue felt pleased. This might be a pleasant encounter after all.

'Now,' Dermot continued, 'if you would like to relieve me of these flowers, I'll open the champagne. Have you got some glasses?'

'Not proper champagne ones, I'm afraid. Will these do?'

'Of course. I've even drunk it out of paper cups on the odd occasion,' he said with a charm that made Sue wonder how genuine he really was.

He poured the drinks with the skill of practice and handed her a glass.

'Here's to new neighbours,' he toasted.

'To new neighbours,' she complied.

A loud barking from the dogs outside interrupted them. William rose, his hackles high along the back of his neck. He gave a low growl.

'Oh, dear, now what's going on?' Sue said a trifle crossly. 'I'd better go and see. Excuse me, will you?'

She went into the yard but could see

nothing unusual. She glanced over to the field and saw a dark shape slinking off. She went back inside.

'Just a fox visiting. I expect he was looking for a free meal.'

Her voice tailed away. Dermot was no longer in the kitchen.

'Dermot,' she called, and he appeared from the sitting-room.

'Sorry. I was looking out of the window to see what was wrong. You still have a lot of work ahead, haven't you?'

'I'm certainly not ready for visitors' inspection,' she said, feeling slightly annoyed with his presumptuousness.

Her stomach gave a huge rumble at this point. If Dermot heard, he made no comment. She had forgotten all about eating, she realised, and her stomach was making its protest. She had nothing in to offer her guest and hoped he would go before her hunger became too obvious. Then she remembered the savouries. She had forgotten. At least that would be something to soak up the wine. She must not get tipsy — that would never do! She delved into the cupboard and brought out the crisps and peanuts. She pulled them open and tipped them into cereal bowls.

'Have something to eat,' she suggested.

'I won't thanks. Don't want to spoil dinner.'

Sue blushed slightly. She couldn't think of anything to say that would seem appropriate. Maybe he had something cooking at home. Why should she feel uncomfortable? He had only come for a drink after all. She stuffed a handful of peanuts into her mouth and chewed on them hungrily. He might have a dinner to return to but she faced a sandwich, at best.

'Look, I don't know if you have any plans, but I was going to try out that little restaurant on the Truro road. Would you like to come with me? I hate eating alone.'

'Isn't it a bit posh?' Sue blurted out without thinking.

‘I’m not sure, but I’ve heard the food is good. Well, what do you say?’

‘It’s very kind of you. Yes, why not?’

It had been a long time since she had been to a really good restaurant. Since coming to Cornwall, she had been forced to count every penny. She and Andy usually went for simple bar snacks.

‘I’d better go and tidy up a bit. I’m a bit scruffy.’

‘Don’t worry, you’ll do fine as you are.’

It turned into a very pleasant evening. Dermot was amusing and entertained her with stories of his past life. It was almost eleven o’clock by the time they returned to the cottage.

‘Thanks very much. I really enjoyed myself,’ Sue told him. ‘I have to make my last check on the dogs, so you can drop me off here. Be easier for you to turn.’

‘You have to go out to the kennels at night? I’m surprised you don’t have closed-circuit television.’

‘Oh, yes, that would be lovely. I can’t even afford to make the cottage habitable so we’re a long way off something like that.’

She pulled a wry face as she spoke. Closed-circuit television? Whatever next? Some folks had strange ideas about money, especially when they had more than they needed.

‘Doesn’t cost all that much. Still, you know best. I’ve enjoyed the evening. We’ll do it again sometime. ’Bye. I’ll be away for a while so will give you a call when I’m back.’

He started up the engine and drove away before Sue could say anything more.

She looked around her tiny kitchen, trying to see it as a stranger might. It was cosy and homely and she loved it. The bouquet of flowers was still in the sink. She searched around, looking for something to put them in. She didn’t even have a vase. A plastic basin was hardly appropriate for such beautiful blooms but it was the best she could do.

They must have cost as much as she usually spent on food for a week, she realised. With the ghost of a sigh, she snapped off the light and went upstairs, William behind her.

'Sorry I left you, William,' she whispered as they both settled down in their beds. 'Mr Dermot Williams is certainly an interesting man, though I imagine he could be somewhat ruthless when the need arose.'

She was soon to discover just how ruthless he could be.

6

It was almost the end of June. In a couple of weeks, her mother was to move into the cottage. For ages, Sue had been busily decorating and trying to clean the rest of the rooms in the cottage. Andy had, as ever, helped in every way possible. They had worked together, plastering and making good the walls and floors. The roof had been fixed so the rain no longer found its way in. Though it might have been desirable, central heating had been abandoned and second-hand storage heaters used instead.

The loan that Mr Read, the family solicitor, had organised, was almost used up. She had forced Andy to accept some payment for all his work but most of that, he must have spent on taking them out for meals. Sometimes, he would buy odd things for the cottage which he saw in sales or auctions. It was beginning to look very homely and comfortable.

An offer had been made for her parents' house and on the advice of Mr Read, she had accepted on her mother's behalf. In a few months, she would have access to some of the money to finish off her mother's rooms and organise some part-time help for her mother.

'Once Mum's things are here, it should look nice, don't you think?' she said to Andy one evening, as they washed out paint brushes. 'I think supper smells about ready,' she added.

Their friendship had continued to flourish, following the slightly rocky patch when Dermot had taken her out to dinner. Andy had taken a while to come to terms with it. Since that evening, Sue had heard nothing from her neighbour. He had been away, she knew, nevertheless, she was slightly surprised that he had totally ignored her existence, even after his return. But now, the preparations for her mother's arrival took precedence over everything. She continued to be grateful to the ever-loyal Andy. Without him, the whole task would have been totally daunting.

'I've got some beers in the van,' Andy said. 'I'll go and get them, shall I?'

A few moments later he returned, looking slightly puzzled.

'Someone drove down to the gate and turned away when he saw me. Didn't realise I looked so off-putting. Hope it wasn't some potential clients for you.'

'Don't worry. People often come down here for a nosy and then drive off again. Probably trying to decide whether the place is suitable for their precious pooch. Now, how many potatoes for you?'

Sue had arranged for one of the local girls to come in for a couple of hours each afternoon, to help out in the kennels. Michelle, who lived in the village, seemed delighted to do anything she was asked, as long as it had to do with dogs. She came to help exercise the dogs when she finished school. She would have spent every day there over the weekends, too, if her mother hadn't insisted she did some revision.

By the time Sue went to collect her mother, Michelle would know the routine as well as she did herself. By then, Michelle would be finished with her school exams and available until she went back into the sixth form in September. It had all worked out very well and gave Sue that essential relief to allow her to do her work in the cottage.

In no time at all, it seemed, Sue was driving her mother down to her new home and new life. The furniture had been sent on the previous day and Andy had arranged to be there to see it into the cottage. As she cleared the final things from her old home, Sue felt this was truly the end of an era. Though her mother was much improved, she didn't want to face the trauma of the final goodbyes and left it to Sue to clear the old house, for ever.

Sue was surprisingly unemotional about saying her own goodbyes. In her own mind, she had already left. The house seemed devoid of the life she had once known, making everything seem quite unfamiliar. She locked the door and delivered the keys to the estate agent for the very last time.

'Goodbye, Hertfordshire,' she whispered as she drove away.

Apart from forgetting a few words and being a little tongue-tied at times, Mrs Saunders was showing signs of being much more like her old self. She was childishly excited about the trip, behaving as if she were going on holiday. Sue felt slightly anxious. Her mother could demand to be taken back, after a short time. The doctor had warned her that it was quite normal for stroke sufferers to behave somewhat irrationally at times.

'And is Aunt Daisy's place really looking nice now?' she asked for the umpteenth time.

'Lovely, and your room will have all

your own things in it by now. I left someone at the cottage to wait for the removal men. He knows where everything is to go. And you will have your own sitting-room with your television and everything you need.'

Her mother nodded and smiled. Sue had decided to make the dining-room into a second sitting-room, giving each of them a bit of space to do their own thing. It meant Sue could entertain her friends while her mother watched the endless daytime soaps and programmes she loved.

When they finally arrived, Michelle was returning from a dog walk and Andy had put on the kettle, ready for tea. His mother had sent over a batch of scones and a tin of home-made shortbread.

'Is this your gardener, dear?' Mrs Saunders asked when she went in.

'This is Andy, Mum. He's a really good friend of mine.'

'How do you do, young man?' she said, shaking his hand. 'You're very tall, aren't you? Especially in such a small space.'

Andy grinned, his blue eyes dancing.

'Hello, Mrs Saunders. I'm delighted to meet you. And yes, I am tall. It's all the clean Cornish air. Now if you'd like to sit down, I'll make some tea.'

'Thank you, dear. I want to have a look round first. I haven't been here since I was a girl. This is my sister's place, you know, Daisy. Remind me Sue, does she still live here?'

Sue smiled but said nothing. She was fascinated to see how her mother would behave with a stranger. She watched as Andy took her arm and led her into the sitting-room.

'This is your own room,' he said. 'See? All your favourite things from your old house. I can move them if you would like them somewhere else.'

'No. It's perfectly charming. Don't you think so, Sue?'

Sue heaved a sigh of relief. So far, so good. Michelle knocked at the back door to say she had finished her tasks for the day.

'Thanks,' Sue said gratefully. 'See you in the morning, if that's OK.'

'Great,' Michelle replied. 'I love coming here. Any time, just ask.'

Though things were going well so far, Sue was aware that everything could turn at any moment. She wanted to make sure that time was available for anything, should she need it. By the time Michelle was back at school in September, the home and business should be running smoothly.

'Where's William, dear?' Mrs Saunders asked. 'He's usually right beside you. I haven't even seen him since I arrived.'

In all the turmoil, Sue realised she hadn't seen him herself, once he'd got over his first ecstatic greetings.

'I expect he's gone exploring,' she said easily.

It was slightly unusual for him to go off for so long but then things were not quite normal at present.

'He's been visiting your neighbour, I think,' Andy said. 'He was there yesterday anyhow. The garden is being landscaped and William seems to like all the activity. One of the workmen has a dog and they were playing together.'

'As long as no one minds,' Sue said uncertainly.

All the same, she went outside and called the dog. It was some minutes later that he arrived, covered in mud and looking very pleased with himself.

'William, what have you been doing? You look like a mud pie. You'll have to be bathed before you come inside.'

She dragged him over to what Andy called the dog's bathroom. He seemed to know what was about to happen and resisted. An unwilling setter was no easy matter to drag across the yard! In the kennel building, there was a shower unit and a clever blow-drying machine. Ingeniously, Andy had built it from various odd bits and pieces. It made the perfect way of cleaning and drying the dogs when they got wet outside. Some owners even asked for their dogs to be bathed before their return.

She had even considered offering it as a regular service. Selling pet foods and bathing and grooming would make a useful addition to her income. For now though, it was a useful way of cleaning up her own, large, excited dog.

It took only a few days for Sue and her mother to get into a routine. Mrs Saunders stayed in bed until Sue had done the early chores, letting the dogs out and feeding them. Mother and daughter then had breakfast together. The business was looking up. Sue had booked every single kennel out for several weeks and was still getting requests for more dogs to be boarded. She told her mother the good news over breakfast one morning.

'My reputation must be getting known,' Sue said happily. 'I've had to say no to half a dozen people in the last few days.'

'Why don't you expand?' her mother said, very rational this morning.

'I'd like to but I don't think the bank would like it.'

‘Use Daddy’s money. There’s plenty, isn’t there? Seems pointless saving it, if you can use it. As long as it doesn’t simply mean you have to work even harder.’

Sue stared at her mother. It would certainly be a good solution but she dared not risk using up her mother’s capital, in case she needed more care in the future. On the other hand, if it was just a loan, once the business increased its turnover, she could pay it back.

‘Maybe I should talk to Andy. He can advise me on what the plan would cost. Then I could have a loan and pay it back as soon as I could. How does that sound?’

‘Do it, Sue. I don’t say it often, but I am so grateful to you for looking after me so well. I was dreading that I might have to stay in that nursing home for the rest of my days.’

‘Oh, Mum, it’s so good to have you here.’

Sue kneeled beside her mother and gave her a hug. She was interrupted by the telephone.

'More customers, do you think?'

The answering machine took the call and she heard a familiar voice booming into the room.

'Sue, please control that dratted dog of yours, will you? He's forever in my garden and digging great holes right where my gardeners are trying to work. I shall be sending you a bill for damaged plants in the next few days, unless you keep him in.'

Before she could get to it, Dermot slammed his own phone down.

'Blast,' she muttered. 'Look, Mum, I'll have to go. You go and read the paper for the moment. I'll clear up the breakfast things later.'

She got up quickly and went in search of her beloved William. He was nowhere to be found in the yard or garden. Somehow, he must have got out and into Dermot's garden. The man had sounded furious, not at all like the charming man who had entertained her to dinner and brought flowers and champagne.

She walked round to her neighbour's house. She had never been close to it before. It was a lovely, old, stone-built farmhouse, with a wide sweep of drive leading to the solid oak front door. Roses and wisteria vied to make the best display and the front garden was already looking a picture. At the side of the house, a huge stretch of new lawn had been laid, with flowering bushes and young trees dotted everywhere.

A small group of workmen stood watching the mad capering of William, as he darted and went down on his front paws, barking madly. Whenever one of them chased him, he tore off the other way, having a wonderful time. He crashed into bushes and scrabbled madly with his paws at the new, young, undoubtedly expensive turf. With a face like thunder, Dermot rushed towards her.

'Call in your blasted dog,' he demanded. 'I'll sue you, I vow it. Nothing but trouble. Get him off my land. Look at him now. Destructive beast. Get rid of him.'

'If you will kindly stop shouting, I shall be able to call him to me. Doesn't any of you know the first thing about dogs? If you shout and run at him like that, he thinks it's a game and he is happy to play with you.'

She turned to her dog and sharply, authoritatively, called his name. Immediately the dog came to her and sat at her feet, panting heavily. He looked up at Dermot with a hurt expression.

'Get him out of my sight,' Dermot snapped. 'And I mean it. If he gets into my garden again, I shall sue you for any damage, if I haven't decided to shoot him first.'

Sue blanched. How could he be such a beast? He had seemed so nice at first but now, Dermot Williams was some sort of monster. White with anger and through gritted teeth, she spoke again.

'Don't worry, Mr Williams, you won't be troubled by Wills again. I'll make sure my fences are secure.'

'See you do. And try to keep your

dogs quiet, will you? The din is quite intolerable at times. I have to work at home, you know.'

Sue stared at the man in shocked surprise. Admittedly, her doggie guests did bark occasionally, especially in the mornings, when she first arrived to let them out. But the rest of the day, they were usually very good. She felt her temper rising and was about to tell him what she thought but caution kicked in. She must not alienate him. He was her neighbour after all and seemed like a pretty powerful man. Besides, if Wills stepped our of line once more, who could tell what Mr Dermot Williams might do? She bit her lip fiercely to stop herself from saying more than she should. She turned and walked back down the drive, holding firmly on to the Irish setter's collar. No one was going to separate her from her best friend.

When she recounted her tale to Andy, later that day, immediately he offered to help her to fix the fences.

'We can probably get away with

patching the wire netting,' he suggested. 'There can only be a few places where he might have got out. What we need to do is to make some system for keeping William inside the kennel area. His easiest route out is straight up your drive. He only has to leap over the little gate and the outside world is his.'

For the rest of the evening, the two of them worked together. They went all round the edge of the field, checking and pushing the fence to look for escape holes. Wills was very excited with all the activity and actually showed them one or two of the weak spots when he scrabbled through.

'I take it your Mr Williams is slightly less charming after all this,' Andy asked, slightly tongue in cheek.

'He's quite an odious man, in my book. I don't even want to think of him. Fancy saying he would shoot Wills. It doesn't bear thinking about. I can't imagine how I could have spent a whole evening with him. I'm not usually such a poor judge of character.'

Andy said nothing but a smile curled round his mouth for the rest of the night.

'How about going out for dinner tomorrow? I can get Mum to come and sit with your mother. Something special?'

'It's very sweet of you, Andy,' Sue said. 'But I'm not sure it's a good idea. I don't think it would be fair to call on your mum. She's done so much for me already.'

'She won't mind. Dad's working away, all this week. She'd probably be glad of the company.'

'Well, if you're sure,' Sue replied.

She didn't know how to turn him down without hurting his feelings. She wanted to remain good friends but, as always, felt certain that he had a different agenda. So far, she had coped with it by never allowing them any opportunities to be totally alone.

'Great. We'll dress up and go somewhere nice. We haven't even been for a bar snack together, not since your mother came down. I shall look forward to tomorrow evening, Sue. It will be great to have you all to myself for once.'

'Thanks, Andy, for everything. I'd never have managed without you. You've been a wonderful friend.'

She gave him a quick hug before she pulled away and went quickly back to the house.

7

After a rather restless night, Sue overslept the following morning. She rushed out to the kennels to let out her charges, planning to feed them a little later, once she had organised her mother's breakfast. She was about to go into the kitchen when she was confronted by a furious Dermot.

'This is it. I've had it with you and your wretched animal. Don't even try to deny it. The evidence is strewn all over your front drive. You'll be receiving a letter from my solicitor.'

He turned and stamped back up the drive, leaving Sue staring after him, totally bewildered.

She pushed open the gate to see what he was talking about. All over the driveway lay plants, bushes and damaged roots. Not only had they been torn out of the ground but most of them were broken, snapped right in the middle. Even if they were to be re-planted, they were too far gone. She almost wept. How could William have possibly done such a huge amount of damage? More to the point, when had he done it?

He had slept the night in her own bedroom, as usual. She had been awake for much of the night, tossing and turning. She had been thinking about Andy and her feeling for him. She had given some worried thought to the problems with Dermot himself and the damage William was supposed to have caused in his garden the previous day. Now, it seemed, her worst fears were realised. Somehow, the dog must have got out and continued his activities. Still puzzled and worried half out of her mind, she went into the kitchen. With everything else, she was not in the mood to discover that her mother was having one of her bad days.

'Where have you been, Sue? It's almost lunchtime and you haven't even given me breakfast. And that girl's gone missing. Sally, isn't she? She hasn't even washed up last night's supper things. Where is she? Staff today are quite useless.'

'I'm sorry, Mum. I'll get you some breakfast right away. And who's this Sally you are talking about?'

'She's some village girl my mother brought in to help with the cooking. Useless, she is. Hasn't got the first idea. Can we have grilled kidneys today? I fancy something tasty.'

Sue sighed. Sally must have been the maid in her grandparents' home, 'way before her own mother had left home. She doubted that grilled kidneys would have been on the menu, even in those far-off days.

'I'll make you some toast, Mum. I'm very busy today. There's a lot to sort out. Now, why don't you sit down there and I'll pour you a nice glass of orange juice?'

'Thank you, dear. Is your father up yet? I couldn't find him in the bed this morning.'

Sue let her mother ramble on. She was too preoccupied to listen or even to respond to her mother. How on earth could William have got out during the night, without her hearing him clattering round? She thought back. She did remember him growling gently at some point during the night, but he often growled in his sleep, as he dreamed. It was so normal, she hadn't given it a thought. All the same, she couldn't risk him being loose during the day and much to his disgust, she shut him in one of the runs while she dealt with her morning chores.

After the dogs were fed and the kennels hosed out, she had to face the mess outside in the drive. Despite his howls, William was left firmly locked up while she scooped up the broken plants and bushes. There were one or two labels still tied to stems and she read them not recognising any of the names. They must be something rare and doubtless, very expensive. She saw her plans for extensions disappearing into the cost of rare plants and lawyers' fees. Dermot would certainly have the best solicitors with the highest price tags. That was his style.

'I'll have to have a collection tin. Lawyers In Need Week,' she muttered angrily.

All the same, she couldn't help puzzling over the logistics of the damage William had caused. Where and how had he got out? When Andy phoned at lunchtime, she had quite forgotten about their planned evening out.

'Can we leave it for another time?' she begged. 'I'm just not in the mood. Besides, Mum is in a funny mood today. I don't like to leave her with anyone.'

'Whatever's gone wrong? You sound awful,' Andy said kindly.

Unusually for her, Sue suddenly burst into tears. It was probably the result of her sleepless night, she told herself. All the same, Andy was most upset and rushed round as soon as he had finished work for the day. Anger had replaced tears by this time and Sue was her usual bouncy self again.

'You see, I know it couldn't have been William. Someone else's dog must have been there. One of the workmen had a dog. It might have been his. I've got to find out, to clear Wills' name. I couldn't bear it if he was hurt by someone.'

'Where is he now?' Andy asked, suddenly afraid.

There was a great deal of barking going on.

'He's locked in one of the spare runs. I know he's pretty cross about it but he has to stay inside until things have calmed down. And to think, only yesterday I was making plans for extending the kennel building. Now I'm probably going to go bust due to legal fees. It isn't fair that someone with so much money as he obviously has could be so mean.'

That night, Sue made absolutely certain that William was locked firmly inside her room and that the doors were also locked. She even made an extra round of the kennels, to make certain that none of the other dogs could possibly get out. She knew there was no way they could, but she was determined to cover herself in every way possible.

When the post arrived the next day, the heavy, official-looking envelope brought dread to her heart. She ripped it open and scanned the letter from Dermot's solicitor. She sat down, feeling sick. Not only was she being sued for damages to the garden and for noise nuisance but worst of all, she was required to vacate the field to the side of her property. Though she had known it was only leased, through an agency, she had not realised that it was Dermot who owned it.

The lease was due to expire in two months and, according to the letter, would not be renewed. It seemed like a death blow to the kennels that she and her aunt before her had worked so hard to build up. Without the field for exercising the dogs, she would find it impossible to continue. She would not have that vital space to let the dogs run free for a period each day.

When Andy arrived later, once more she poured out all her troubles.

'So, there it is. Without the field, I might as well give up right now.'

'You can't, Sue. You simply can't play into his hands. We can get round it somehow. Now look. I drew up some plans for you, for the extension you were talking about. It really won't cost very much at all.'

'There's no way I can even think of extending, not now. Thanks, Andy, but you can forget it.'

'What do other kennels do for exercise areas? Town kennels for example. I can't believe they all have huge areas like this. The dogs will have to have longer walks less often. You can rely on the runs more for each dog. Come on now. This isn't the Sue we all know and love.'

He may only have been quoting a

saying, a platitude, but when Sue heard the word love, she froze. It was as if she had been hit hard. Andy must not love her. It was wrong. But at least it had served to bring her back to her usual self.

'You are right, of course. The field was convenient though not essential. I shall have to spend even more time walking the dogs each day. S'pose it will keep me fit.'

She picked up Andy's sketches for the extension. It would mean planning permission and everyone would have the chance to voice their objections. She could just imagine whose voice would be shouting the loudest.

Over the next week or so, bookings suddenly began to drop. Sue found it hard to believe that it was pure coincidence. She felt very relieved that she had done nothing further towards her extension plans. At least no more money had been committed to a potentially useless project. Try as she might, she could find no reason for the fall-off in trade.

Fortunately, her mother was having a good patch, so Sue was able to concentrate on her work. She felt worried that future bookings were so low. This was the height of the holiday season but come September, things were looking extremely gloomy. When she mentioned her worries to Andy, he suggested that she should advertise.

'But I have adverts everywhere I can think of. Campsites, hotels and even some of the local theme parks. Where else is there? Apart from the national magazines and they cost a fortune for even a few column inches.'

'The Internet, of course,' Andy replied. 'It's obvious. You need a website with a few pictures of the kennels, the dogs and the beaches. It has to be a winner.'

'I know as much about the Internet as I do about fishing. I wouldn't know where to start. Besides, my computer is about as old as you get. I doubt it is even capable of doing anything more than running my booking system.'

'Think about it,' Andy suggested. 'I have to go now. It's the surfing championships this weekend. I must get a bit of practice. Are you coming down to watch us?'

'I'll try to get down on Sunday. So you'd better make the finals or I'll miss out. Saturday is change-over day so I'll be up to my eyes. Michelle will be there to cheer you on.'

When he had gone, Sue decided to take William for a run. He had been locked firmly inside the gates for several days. At least there had been no more incidents with plants since last week, so it had been worth it. William was most unhappy at being away from his mistress for such long periods. He couldn't work out what he had done wrong.

The following weekend, in a rare moment's peace, Sue read the local paper. There were several adverts for computer companies, including one which offered a service to build websites for people who had neither skill nor time to do them for themselves. She cut the page out and decided she might try to phone them the next week. It might be worth knowing what it would cost at least.

She heard her mother's voice calling and put the paper down. Moments of quiet were all too rare these days. She listened to what her mother was saying. It sounded like utter gibberish. Sue sighed. The rational days seemed to be getting less and there were more and more of the difficult days. Today was one she could well do without. With a sigh, she went to investigate.

After lunch the next day, Sue took her dog down to the edge of the beach to watch the championship surfers. It was down to the last five, Andy among them. Most of the other contestants came from other parts of the country, so the local support was all with Andy. The usual crowd of girls was out in front, yelling and shouting. The waves were rising and getting quite rough. It had to give the local man an advantage and he was certainly making the most of every chance.

It was soon down to the last two. They were neck and neck. A huge wave came. Both contestants went for it and both rose to their feet on their boards. Andy rode right into the beach and the other man fell just before. The crowd went wild. The local man had won. Sue was cheering with the rest, from her perch above the beach. William's tail was wagging, as if he, too, understood the excitement. Andy spotted her and waved the cup triumphantly above his head. He beckoned but she could not take Wills on to the beach. She shook her head, hoping he understood.

When the fun was over, she went back to her cottage. She had left her mother sleeping in front of the television, as she often did. Sue called to her as she went into the kitchen.

'Are you awake, Mum? Would you like a cup of tea?'

There was silence. Sue knocked at

her mother's door and looked in. The room was empty. She looked upstairs and in the bathroom, everywhere. There was no sign of her! Sue felt a small knot of panic beginning to rise. Her mother had never tried to leave the house before, unless someone was with her. Then she heard an unaccustomed barking, much more than usual.

She ran out to the kennels and saw that the door was wide open. There was a screen door inside so that Sue could work when it was hot, leaving the main door ajar. Now, everything was open. She went in quietly, so as not to cause any panic. Her mother was standing outside one of the runs, talking to the occupant, a golden Labrador.

'So you see, you poor dear, this nasty man has stopped my daughter from taking you in the field. Don't worry though. I'm sure she will be back soon. Then you can go on the beach. Oh, Sue. There you are. Do you know this poor boy hasn't had a walk for days? He told me so himself.'

'It's all right, Mum. Come on into the house now. The kettle will be boiling and we'll have a cup of tea.'

'But the dog . . . '

'It's all right. I'll see to him in a little while. Come and have some tea.'

Sue felt a heavy depression settling over her. Times like this made her feel so helpless. She had to run her business and make a success of it, for both their sakes.

As soon as she had a spare moment the next day, she telephoned the computer company about a website. If it wasn't too expensive, she would try it as a way of getting publicity. The girl at the other end would give no details about costs. She finally persuaded Sue to allow a rep to call, promising that he would be able to give her all the prices and information she needed.

'He'll be in your area this afternoon, if that's not too soon,' the girl said.

'OK. Might as well get it moving. I've only got an old computer though.'

'Don't worry, madam. We can even

supply you with a new machine, or come to some arrangement. Our Mr Johnson will be with you around three, if that's convenient.'

After lunch, Sue settled the dogs outside and her mother in front of the television. She gave a grin. Young mothers were criticised for leaving babies and toddlers for hours in front of the television and here she was, doing the same thing with her mother. She planned to meet the rep in the office, where he could see her old machine for himself. She wondered if she ought to offer him some tea but that meant going back into the house and disturbing her mother.

At three o'clock sharp her loud, outside bell rang. She went out of the office to the gate and immediately her heart sank. Dermot was standing there, briefcase in hand and looking immaculate in tan slacks and a cream linen shirt. She wondered rashly where William was.

'What do you want?' she challenged.

'William is safely locked away.'

'You asked for help with a computer. I'm here to help.'

'But the girl said it was a Mr Johnson who would be calling.'

'Bill Johnson was called away. Unavoidable. I'm here instead.'

'But surely you aren't a rep. I mean, you are the owner of the company, aren't you?'

'Doesn't do me any harm to make a few calls. Helps me to keep abreast of things. Now, are you going to let me in or shall I go away?'

'You'd better come in.'

She felt hairs prickling the back of her neck as he followed her into the little office. His masculine scent came with him and she felt herself suddenly going weak at the knees. Drat the man. He had put some weird kind of spell on her. He glanced round the office and saw the elderly computer sitting on the desk. He looked at her and began to grin.

'You don't mean to say this is it? You

aren't serious, of course. This machine is not even capable of going on-line.'

'I told the girl it was an old machine but she said not to worry. You could come up with something, an arrangement of some sort.'

'I suspect that most of our deals are 'way out of reach.'

'So why are you here?'

'Curiosity, interest. I like you, Sue. You are different from most of the women I know.'

'You've a funny way of showing it. All your threats and solicitors and everything. You want to put me out of business so why should you try to help me?'

'I do like you. I don't like your noisy dogs and, you have to admit, you've caused me a great deal of inconvenience and damage. Your dog is quite out of control and you seem to do nothing about it.'

'How dare you! My dog is perfectly well trained. He's never been out of my sight for days. He is locked up whenever I have to leave the house and I assure you, he's never been out at night. You are blaming the wrong person. Wrong dog.'

Dermot watched her and frowned. His mouth tightened and he rose from his seat.

'Am I? Are you quite sure about that? Come out here and look at the latest damage. I've got the evidence right in my car boot. Come on.'

He grabbed her wrist and forced her to go with him.

'Explain this lot,' he almost shouted, pointing into his car. 'These were all imported specimens. I paid forty pounds for this one, fifty-eight for this one. These smaller plants were brought in from South America, a collection that is probably unrepeatable. You're looking at a total loss of hundreds of pounds here.'

Blazing with anger, he pulled them all out of his car and dumped them unceremoniously on the path.

'You might as well keep them. If your

dog wants to chew them to pieces you might as well let him. You are going to pay for them anyway.'

'Dermot, please listen. It couldn't have been William. Really it couldn't.'

'I don't want to hear any more. I'll send you the bill.'

He climbed into his car and drove away, swishing the gravel unnecessarily out of his path. She watched him disappear, her eyes filling with tears of anger and injustice.

'Was that the gardener, dear?' Mrs Saunders asked. 'I'm so glad he came. I couldn't manage to carry all the plants home myself, not in the dark.'

Sue stared at her mother. The sickening truth dawned on her. It hadn't been William destroying her neighbour's garden, although the culprit had almost certainly come from her own house.

8

Sue didn't want to upset her mum but she had to get to the bottom of this and straighten out the whole affair with Dermot.

'Did you go out in the night, Mum?' she asked gently when they were back inside.

'It's wonderful that the nursery was open so late, wasn't it, dear? Such lovely plants. Your father will be so pleased when he comes back from . . . now, where was it? Where did he go? I keep forgetting.'

'Oh, Mum,' Sue whispered.

It was obvious that she had been living in a false sense of security. She would have to get someone in to look after her mother, especially when she had to go out somewhere. Even looking after the business required her to be out of sight of her mother for much of the day.

Certainly, she needed to change the type of locks on the doors. Maybe if she had one which required a key to open it, that would help. She even contemplated some sort of alarm that would sound if a door or window was opened. How did other people manage, she wondered. Obviously, she owed Dermot Williams some sort of explanation and she also had to pay for his damaged plants.

For once, Andy did not come round after he had finished work. She missed him. Sue had been planning to ask him about locks and alarms but she would have to wait. She felt tense and edgy and could not concentrate on the television programme she was watching with her mother.

'I'm just going to give William a short walk,' she said at last. 'Promise you will stay and watch the end of this programme. I shall be back before it finishes to make your cocoa.'

Mrs Saunders waved her hand, as if waving her off. Deep in thought, Sue strode down the lane that led into the village. The lights were all on at Andy's place and impulsively, she knocked at the door.

'Hello, dear,' Alice said. 'Lovely to see you. How are you getting on? I've been meaning to call on your mother but I've been that busy lately.'

'Nice to see you, too. I wondered if Andy's at home. I need to ask him a few things.'

'Come inside. He's out somewhere this evening. I thought he was with you actually but I must have got it wrong. Can I help?'

Sue hesitated before deciding to pour out the whole sorry tale.

'So you see, I'm at my wits' end. I don't know what to do for the best. Mum's very happy but she gets so muddled. When something like this happens, I see that she can't be left alone for such long periods of time.'

'I could always come in to sit with her, when you have to go out to the town or something,' Alice offered.

'That's really kind of you but I know how busy you are yourself. Besides, I need something more organised than relying on your kindness all the time. The problem is that I couldn't afford to pay anyone, not the way things are at present. By the time I've paid for the damage to my neighbour's garden, the coffers will be quite empty, and just when trade was beginning to pick up.'

'I'll call round tomorrow,' Alice insisted. 'We can have a chat and see if there's something we can come up with.'

'You are wonderful,' Sue said gratefully.

Alice knew everyone in the village and would probably be able to make some suggestions at least.

'I'd better get home now. Mum's programme will be finishing and I daren't risk any more mishaps. Thanks for listening and for being so concerned.'

'What are friends for? I'll tell Andy you called. No doubt he'll be round tomorrow sometime.'

Once her mother was in bed and her final rounds were completed, Sue locked the front and back doors securely. She put a chair in front of each, wedging them below the handle. If her mother tried to get out, she would make a noise and surely wake her or William. It was all so distressing and beyond her experience. How could she stop her mother from doing silly things and yet still give her some respect and independence?

It was a peaceful night, though Sue jolted awake several times. Whenever a floorboard creaked or a sound outside made William growl softly, she was wide awake, trying to hear if her mother was moving about. But she seemed to have slept heavily and was very cheerful and normal the next morning.

'The postman's here, Sue,' she called.

Sue dried her hands on the kitchen towel and went to the door.

'Mornin',' the postman said cheerfully. 'Got one to sign for, just there.

That's it. Lovely day, isn't it?'

'Great,' Sue replied automatically.

She didn't like the look of the envelope she had signed for. It was bulky, recorded delivery. Surely it was too soon to be another letter from Dermot's solicitor. But then, he had them all at his beck and call at all hours so that's what it must be. she opened it and slumped down.

It was worse than she'd expected. There were more complaints about noise; a claim for compensation for the damaged plants; reimbursement for the cost of the gardeners who had put them in and finally a massive claim for compensation for inconvenience. How dare he? Sue was struggling to make a living and he was rolling in money. It would be peanuts to him but it was more than she had in the world.

She'd show him! In a fury, she grabbed her cheque book and wrote out the required amount. There was no way it wouldn't bounce but she didn't care. He could take her to court sometime in the future but at least she would have the satisfaction of throwing it at him now.

'I'm going out, Mum. Don't leave the house, for anything at all. Do you understand?'

'Of course, dear,' Mrs Saunders said meekly. 'I don't have to go shopping today, do I?'

'No, Mum. You just stay there. Watch television or something.'

Sue stormed up the drive, leaving William safely locked away. The sight of the Irish setter would have only aggravated the situation. She walked briskly and angrily down Dermot's drive and thumped on his door. A woman answered.

'I want to see Mr Williams,' Sue demanded.

'I'm not sure if he's home,' the woman began.

'He is, and I'll find him myself, thank you.'

She pushed past the woman and stamped down the hallway.

'One moment, whoever you are. There's no need for such rudeness.'

The poor woman was floundering.

'Yes, there is. Your employer needs to be told that he can't stamp on just anyone less fortunate than himself. Is this his study?' she asked, pushing one of the doors open.

The housekeeper rushed after the visitor, trying to get to Dermot first.

'I don't think he needs you to protect him. Not when he has everyone else in his pocket,' Sue shouted angrily.

'Can I help you, Miss Saunders?' the ultra-calm voice of Dermot Williams said.

'This letter you sent. How dare you demand so much money? You know how broke I am.'

'It's fair recompense for the damage and inconvenience. I don't think it's at all unreasonable. I have to wait for new plants to be brought in and then pay for them all to be planted. Surely you see how reasonable I am being. I could demand that your dog be destroyed. He is quite out of control, that much is obvious.'

'My dog is not out of control, nor was he responsible for the damage,' Sue hissed.

'Then why are you waving that cheque around? Presumably you have come to pay me, though my solicitor would have expected you to send it directly to her.'

'I want you to know exactly what it means to me. When you pay this cheque into your overloaded account, it will probably bounce. My business will probably be closed down and I shall be left with a home I can't afford and a sick mother to care for. I can't even afford proper care for her now. If I use up her own money, there will be nothing left when she has to go into full-time care. When I look round here at what you have, it's quite obvious you have absolutely no need of my hard-earned money. That collection of china figurines alone must be worth twice as much as I own in my entire property.'

‘They are nice, aren’t they?’ Dermot said irritatingly.

Sue was quite ready to throw several of the lovely pieces right at him. Sensing her thoughts, he jumped up from his seat and placed himself between her and the china.

‘I think you need to calm down a little. Mrs Bannister will make us some coffee and we can discuss this.’

Sue turned to see the housekeeper still standing at the door. She was thoroughly enjoying the exchange and doubtless saving up the story to spread round the village later. She slipped out, presumably to make coffee. Not that Sue was in any state to sit and drink coffee, especially with this awful man. She was rational enough to realise that some sort of discussion would be to her own advantage in the long run.

He reached for her arm and led her to a comfortable, leather armchair. She stared at his hand on her arm, wondering how and why he had such a profound effect on her. She still remembered the electricity that had shot between them at their earlier meeting. How could she even remotely like someone who could treat her the way he had?

'Miss Saunders, Sue, I'm sorry to cause you such problems but you must see how angry I was. I had barely finished the planting before your dog came ripping through my garden. I have paid a great deal of money for landscaping to fit in with the area. I have guests coming to stay very soon and I had hoped to have everything finished before then.'

'I wouldn't have thought rare plants brought in from abroad were exactly fitting for Cornwall. What's wrong with the natural things that grow here? At least you can be certain they will grow in this climate.'

He stared at Sue.

'I never thought of it like that. I'm not much of a gardener. I've always lived in cities. It seemed like the right thing to do. The chap who designed it was an old friend. I just took his word for it. Ah, Mrs Bannister, our coffee.'

He remained silent as the housekeeper poured and served their drinks. She offered biscuits, which Sue declined.

'Thanks. That will be all,' Dermot said.

Mrs Bannister looked disappointed but left the room, pulling the door to behind her. Sue sipped the drink, using the quiet moment to try and regain her composure. She knew she had behaved irrationally but anger had driven her. Foolishly, her actions had made it look as if she accepted responsibility for the damage. If she defended her dog too much, the sad truth about her mother would become public knowledge. The easiest way to keep things quiet was after all admission of guilt and to pay up.

'Maybe we can come to some agreement,' Dermot said calmly. 'I don't mean you to go out of business, of course, but I am entitled to some recompense, you must admit. I'll forget about replacing the actual plants and you can pay for the labour. I might take up your suggestion of using local plants. That would be less expensive, anyhow.'

What an unusual silver grey his eyes were, Sue was thinking. Like the sun shining on the sea when it creeps from under grey clouds. She pulled her thoughts back. What on earth was she doing mooning over this man? He was her sworn enemy, the man she had to challenge at every step.

'Thanks,' she stammered, wondering what on earth he had said.

He interested her. What was someone so successful, so good-looking and charming doing here in a remote village in Cornwall? He was a city man, used to travelling all round the world, no doubt. The house breathed wealth, elegance and good taste in every bit she had seen.

'You must admit, the dogs do make a racket,' he was saying. 'I do feel justified in claiming compensation for the noise.

But as you suggest, what's the point of complaining and going through endless court appearances, if you haven't any money and will be closing down anyway? Just listen to them at the moment.'

'They are barking rather a lot, and it's actually most unusual. Maybe someone has got into the kennels. The dogs never make this much noise as a rule.'

'I agree. Come on. Maybe something's wrong.'

He went through the door, barely holding the door long enough for her to pass in front of him. He headed off down the drive and into hers. She could scarcely keep up with him. The barking reached a crescendo as they got there. There were dogs everywhere, in the main exercise run, in the garden, in the yard. Some were fighting and others simply diving into the food bins, gorging on the unexpected feast. William was barking furiously at the back door. The door was pulled slowly back and Mrs Saunders' anxious face peered out.

'Sue,' she wailed. 'Sue, where are you?'

'It's OK, Mum. I'm here. You stay inside. I'll sort it out.'

Quickly, she called William to her side and took his collar. She pushed him inside, knowing the big dog would behave and might even calm her mother. She called one or two of the others and put them back into their runs, shutting the doors behind them. She picked up the hose and turned the tap, ready to squirt any dogs who didn't respond to her call. No way was she going to try to separate any fighting dogs with her bare hands. In minutes, she had everything under control. There were still two dogs racing round the exercise field, but they were playing happily and chasing each other in a friendly way. Dermot was leaning on the gate watching her.

'Congratulations. You certainly have a way with the animals. I thought you'd be facing huge vet bills and even more claims for compensation from angry owners.'

'There may be the odd bit of injury. I shall have to examine them all carefully. Now, if you'll excuse me, I'd better see if I can find out how all of this happened.'

The back door opened again and her mother peered out.

'Is it safe for me to come out yet?' she asked.

William pushed past her and went to lick his mistress.

'Yes. The dogs are all safely out of the way again. How did they get out, Mum?'

'I wanted to help. You have to work so hard, dear. They seemed to want to go out to play so I opened their doors and they all rushed everywhere, before I could stop them. How do you manage to look after so many of them, dear? Oh, your nice new gardener is here. Is he going to put my plants in for me? Where have they gone? I left them all round at the side.'

Dermot stared at the woman and then looked back at Sue.

'I think I may owe an apology to William. It seems it may not have been him after all,' he said.

Sue saw recognition dawn in his eyes and knew he had guessed the truth.

'Look, we need to discuss things. Forget about that letter. I'll speak to my solicitor right away,' he went on.

'Thanks, and thanks for coming with me. It was nice of you.'

'I didn't exactly do much. Besides, I was hardly going to be able to work with that racket going on, was I? He's a handsome dog, your Irish setter. Always were a bit wild that breed. In fact, I'd go so far as to say totally scatty.'

'He is a wonderful dog, just a bit over-enthusiastic at times.'

Dermot turned and walked away.

'Come over this evening if you can spare the time. We'll discuss our next move.'

Sue watched him. He had seemed

reasonably sympathetic to her plight and he admitted that he didn't entirely hate William. He couldn't be all bad, after all. Anyone who liked dogs had some redeeming features.

When Andy arrived to invite her to go for a drink that evening, she poured out the whole sorry story.

'I have to go and see him to discuss some sort of resolution to our problems. Please, could you stay with Mum for a while? I promise I won't be long but it's so important.'

The expression that crossed Andy's face was quite unfathomable. He looked slightly cross, unhappy, anxious, all at the same time. Sue realised what she was asking of him. He wanted to spend time with her and she was going to see someone he saw as his rival.

'Look, it's just to discuss his ridiculous claims. If I don't sort it out, he could put me right out of business. I think I may be able to persuade him to withdraw his claim, even if I do have to crawl a bit.'

'I don't like you going into that spider's lair,' Andy said unhappily. 'I think you should take a witness with you. I could phone my mum and ask her to come and sit, then I can be with you.'

'It's very sweet of you to care, but I'm a big girl now. I can handle this. Don't worry. Now, please will you stay?'

Unhappily, he nodded his head.

9

Sue knocked at the door of the big farmhouse, feeling more than a little trepidation. She was holding tightly to her temper, determined that she would do nothing to jeopardise her future. She would be charm itself, she decided.

'Come in. I've got some wine chilling. You'll stay for dinner, of course. Mrs B is cooking a roast.'

Dermot looked immaculate, as always, and was obviously set to charm her. She smiled, amused that she had realised they were both playing the same game.

'A drink would be nice but I can't possibly stay for dinner. Besides, I am a vegetarian.'

'I didn't know. Mrs B will rustle up something else, I'm sure.'

'I have to get back to my mother.'

'Ah, yes, your mother. I gather she is

rather difficult. We don't want a repeat of this morning's little drama, do we? I suspect she is the cause of several other dramas that have been affecting us lately.'

Sue frowned. She was not going to enter into any such discussions at this moment.

'About your garden. If I buy you some more plants and manage to put them in your garden myself, can we forget about the compensation?'

Sue had been trying to think of ways round her problems all afternoon. She had worked out that if she paid Michelle for a few extra hours, she would have time to do the work next door herself. It would certainly be less expensive in the long run.

'That sounds reasonable,' Dermot agreed. 'But I'd want some say in what plants you choose.'

'Agreed. And the lease on the field? Would you reconsider that? I really do need that space.'

'I'm afraid I have plans for that piece

of land. Actually, it will all be out in the open soon. I'm planning to take on a new venture. I'm converting the barns and outbuildings and plan to build on that land as well. I'm going to make an exclusive complex of holiday homes, probably timeshares. So you see, I can't possibly have a noisy kennels next door.'

Sue sat very still as she listened, the horror growing as she realised all the implications of his words. A holiday complex, here in Nancetowan? It was a ghastly thought. Her voice shook as she spoke.

'But you can't, not here. You'd never get planning permission.'

'But I already have.'

'But no one has been notified. No one has given us the chance to object and believe me, people will object.'

'I doubt it. Most locals will be delighted for the chance to do some real business. I shall become one of the main employers in the area. Believe me, Sue, this will be the making of this little village. Really put it on the map.'

'I don't think the local people want to be on any map, more than we are already. How did you get the planning through, without anyone knowing?'

'It's been in the local papers. That long column that no one ever reads? Small black printing?'

Sue's heart sank even further. Why did people with money have so much power over everyone's lives?

'You'll hate it when everywhere is covered in screaming kids and there are people round every corner.'

'I plan to be away most of the summer. I have a boat and plan to take long trips in it. I shall have a telephone and laptop computer, so I can keep in touch.'

'You've really got it all worked out, haven't you?'

'I think so. I might even have a job for you, when you close the kennels.'

'I shall never give up willingly. You have a fight on your hands. I shall have plenty of objectors on my side. Don't count too many chickens, Mr Williams. I'm not done for yet.'

'I do like a woman with fire and passion. Yes, Sue, I think we may even have a future together.'

She stared at him totally nonplussed. He had to be joking. Close down her business, remove her livelihood and then suggest . . . whatever it was he was suggesting? He had such conceit!

'I have to go. My mother needs me,' she said suddenly.

'Maybe you ought to consider a decent nursing home.'

'Chance would be a fine thing,' she muttered, 'especially if you insist on ruining my business.'

'That sounds a touch like emotional blackmail,' he said dryly.

'You're the expert, I'd say.'

She swept out of his house and back up the drive. Her mind was racing. She couldn't wait to get Andy and everyone on her side. They must surely all hate the idea of a holiday complex in the village. The ambience would be lost for ever and a new character given to the place. But when she told Andy the news, he was quite philosophical about it.

'If it's going ahead anyway, we need to be in at the start. Maybe he will give work to the local people and the village really will benefit.'

'But he wants me out of here. He wants to ruin my business. How can I just give it to him?'

Further conversation was prevented by the arrival of Mrs Saunders, dressed in her coat and hat and apparently, all ready to go shopping.

'I must get some fish for your father's supper. He'll be coming in late tonight so I need something that will cook quickly. See you later, dear. Now, where did I put my car keys?'

With a sigh, Sue began to deal with the situation and persuaded her mother to lie down for a rest. Once in bed, she took her some cocoa before finally dropping into a chair, quite exhausted.

'Your mother ought to go into that

nursing home along the coast, even for a few days,' Andy said.

'Oh, yes, I should think so. Have you any idea what a place like that costs? It's quite impossible, I'm afraid.'

'Surely you can get help with the cost.'

'Not when Mum's got money of her own, above a certain amount. She hasn't got all that much and I feel she needs to hang on to that in case she really has to go in permanently.'

'But you desperately need a break. I think you should look into it, just for a week or two. You could have a loan if you don't want to use up your mum's money.'

Andy stood and put his hand on her shoulder. It felt comforting and warm. She could almost feel his strength pouring into her, giving her own weakness a boost.

'I'll think about it,' she promised.

'Please do. I promise I'll take you out for a super meal the first night you are free. Now, I'd better get going. I said

I'd be back hours ago. Don't worry about things. I'm sure everything will come right soon.'

He dropped a peck on her cheek and left. The room seemed empty without him. Sue felt even more confused. Obviously, the day had taken its toll on her. It had been a difficult few weeks, one way or another.

Sue sighed and made the decision. She needed a few days alone, to get on top of things. Her books needed doing, mail needed replies and the house needed a thorough clean. The nursing home was going to be essential if she was to survive. She phoned the matron. Her mother could stay at Sea Spray for as long as she liked. Anxiously, Sue explained the problems but the matron seemed unperturbed.

'We're quite used to a few little eccentricities, my dear. Don't worry about a thing. Now, when would you like to bring your mother?'

Mrs Saunders fully believed she was going to have a little holiday in a nice hotel and she set off quite happily. She liked her room and waved goodbye to Sue without a care in the world. Sue heaved a sigh of relief and settled down to an evening of catching up.

Soon after work the next day, Andy arrived to accompany Sue to the nursing home. After the visit, they were going out for dinner, as he had promised.

'I really don't know how she'll take to it,' Sue said anxiously.

'We'll soon see. I expect she'll be fine.'

He was quite right. When Sue went into the lounge, she was introduced immediately to all her mother's new friends. Andy was her gardener, but he smiled, happily accepting the title. According to her mother, Sue had paid for this holiday from her highly successful business and wasn't she a good daughter?

'Now, dear, would you like tea? I'll ring for it, if you would. They're very good here. Nothing's too much trouble.'

'I'll bet,' Sue whispered through her teeth.

'Quite the lady, isn't she?' Andy said as they drove away. 'My guess is that she will want to stay there. She's got people to talk to and her meals always on time. Don't get me wrong. I'm not suggesting your meals weren't.'

'It's all right. I know exactly what you mean. No dogs making demands at odd hours, and no running out of bread or milk. And this is nice. You were right. I did need a break. You're such a good friend.'

'Don't you forget it, either. You know I'd like us to be more than friends, don't you?'

'Of course, but the timing's awful. I can't even think of myself and any sort of future at the moment. Now, I thought we were going to eat. I'm starving.'

Mrs Saunders did not want to leave the nursing home. She was comfortable, well-looked after and fully believed in her rôle as a rich lady, staying in an exclusive hotel. She had soon been there for over a month. During these weeks, Sue had worked hard to get the kennels running to the best of her ability. She had discussed things with Dermot on a couple of occasions and they had even established a reasonable understanding with each other. Though they would never agree about some things, he had stopped trying to close her down. In fact, he had even come to realise that her establishment could be of some use to his own venture.

He offered to help with building the other extension she wanted, as long as she would guarantee space for any dogs his future tenants might require. It looked as though things were going to work out.

'How long is your mother going to stay in the nursing home?' Andy asked one evening.

'She'd like to stay for ever but I can't afford much longer. Pity really. She loves it and I can really get on with my work. Still, I always knew it was a temporary arrangement. Even with help, it's much more than I can afford.'

She was to get a surprise the following morning. The usual weekly envelope arrived from the nursing home. When she opened it, ready to write the cheque, there was a receipt for three weeks' payment in advance.

'I don't understand,' she muttered.

Then it became clear. It was obvious. Andy, bless him, had paid for a whole month. She couldn't accept it, though. Immediately, she dialled his number. He sounded as puzzled as she was and insisted he had not paid any bills.

'Don't pretend, Andy. It's really sweet of you but I can't let you. I can't accept charity, and I won't be bought.'

'Don't you think I know that? I wouldn't even try. Believe me, I've wanted to offer to help many times, but I knew exactly what your reaction would be. Look, I'll see you later. I really have to go now.'

Sue turned to the rest of the post. A

now familiar letter from Dermot's solicitor was among the rest. With a heavy sigh, she tore it open. What now, she wondered. Things had seemed to be going well between them. Her jaw dropped as she read the words. Was this her lucky day or what? Mr Williams had decided to drop all his charges and had pleasure in returning her cheque! With everything that had been happening, she'd managed to forget all about the cheque she'd taken round to him. She knew it hadn't been cashed, of course, but she had lost all track of it.

There were more surprises to come. Three more bookings arrived for dogs to be boarded, enclosing deposits. People did not always enclose a deposit and she had to trust to luck and their honesty. She wondered how they had heard of her. She had not been advertising in any of the areas where they had come from. Then she noticed that one person mentioned an excellent website and wished her luck with her new ventures.

There was only one person she knew who had anything to do with such matters — Dermot Williams. He must have produced a website for her. They had scarcely even discussed the matter so he must have really taken matters into his own hands. It may have been kind of him but obviously, there was something in it for him. As soon as she could, she went round to his house.

'I don't expect charity,' she said accusingly. 'I'm quite prepared to pay you for your work. I may not be well-off but I can afford some costs.'

'Don't be silly. It wasn't charity,' Dermot replied.

He was looking especially good this morning, she noticed. He was wearing the usual silk shirt, this time a grey one that exactly matched his eyes. She smoothed her T-shirt, aware of what was lacking in her own appearance, especially compared to him.

'I was pleased to help. Besides, we already agreed, it's in my own interest to have a successful business up and running. I don't want a scruffy rundown sort of place next door. As I've said all along, my complex is going to be an exclusive, expensive set-up.'

'And what about the nursing home bill? Was that you as well?'

'So what if it was? I realised what a dreadful time you've been having and thought it might help you a bit.'

'Why, Dermot? Why have you started to be so rice to me?'

'Would you believe I have fallen head-over-heels for you?'

Sue's eyes widened. Her jaw dropped. This was the last thing she had been expecting. In love? He couldn't be, not with her. She croaked as she said the words.

'Don't be silly,' she said, stunned. 'How could you? I mean why?'

'Come here, Sue. You are really funny. You're a lovely woman. With a bit of care and attention, a few new clothes and a hair make-over, you could match up to anyone, anywhere.'

He reached over to her and pulled

her towards him. When his arms circled her waist, she felt as if she was turning to jelly. She leaned against him, his masculine scent filling her nostrils. He bent his head to kiss her. His lips were soft and gentle, but demanding. She met his demands and responded with an enthusiasm that took even her by surprise. Could this possibly be the magic she had been seeking for so long?

'I want to be with you, Sue. I want us to be together. Come away with me for the weekend. We'll go and stay on my boat, just the two of us. What do you say?'

'I can't possibly. I have a business to run. I can't just walk away from it. Besides what ever would I do with William, and my mother? I must visit her every day.'

'Please think about it. It can be sorted, I'm sure. The dog can stay in your own kennels surely? And your mother won't miss you for a couple of days. Can't your girl look after things?

And your faithful swain, surely he would look in at the kennels for you.'

'Faithful swain? How dare you! Andy is a very dear friend.'

'Is that all he is? A friend?'

'Of course. I'm not the sort of woman who leaps into a relationship with the first man she sees.'

'What about the second man? Do I stand a chance?'

He bent to kiss her again and she pulled away.

'Please, this is all so sudden. I need time to think.'

'I'll call you this evening. I want you, Sue, more than anything. I hope you'll at least give me this chance. Come to my boat with me. You won't be disappointed, I promise you.'

'I'll think about it. But that's all I'm promising for now.'

In a daze, she went back home. She couldn't possibly go away with this man, not alone. What would people think? Besides, she wasn't sure it was what she wanted. It was very tempting, however. A rest from work, if only a couple of days, sounded wonderful. She made some coffee and continued her daydream. William sat with his head resting on her lap. She fondled his soft ears.

'Oh. Wills, what would you tell me to do, if you could? You don't much like Dermot, do you? But he is everything a girl could want. Good-looking, rich, successful.'

Wills growled. There was someone coming down the drive.

'Miss Saunders? Flowers for you.'

The delivery man stood almost hidden behind a massive basket of the most wonderful flowers she had ever seen.

'For me? Whoever . . . '

'There's a card with them. 'Bye for now.'

He had a very knowing grin, as he turned away. Sue seized the card to read the message.

We may not have time to sail to paradise in one weekend but we

might come pretty close.

No wonder the man was grinning. It was a pretty suggestive message in anyone's book. What was she to do?

10

Why don't you come to the pub this evening?' Andy suggested when he called to replace a broken pane of glass in the storeroom. 'You must make the most of your time. You work too hard.'

'Oh, yes? And what about you? You are always doing something for some-one and never asking for payment. You are a real love but you'll never get rich that way.'

'Maybe there's more to life than getting rich,' he said wisely. 'Now, are you going to come out willingly or do I have to be masterful?'

Sue giggled.

'That could be fun. No, I didn't mean it. I'll be delighted to have a break.'

As they drove away, Sue missed the telephone ringing. She saw there was a message when they came back later.

Andy, obviously feeling quite at ease, put the kettle on for coffee and she played back the message, left by Dermot.

'Sue, I'm still waiting for your answer. I'd hoped the flowers might have helped. Ring me when you're back.'

Andy gave her a mug of coffee, his face like thunder.

'And what answer might that be?' he demanded.

'Not that it's your business, but he's invited me on his yacht for the weekend. Thought I needed a break.'

'And the best I can offer is an evening at the local pub. Not much of a comparison, am I? Down, Wills. Seems your mistress has bigger fish to fry.'

William howled as Andy went out of the door. He turned and looked back at her.

'And no, I won't look after Wills for you and nor will I mind your kennels while you're away. In fact, I was thinking of a bit of a change myself. I'm leaving Cornwall for good. I've had enough.'

He strode away and Sue realised she was probably losing the very best friend she had ever had. Sadly, she watched the red van as Andy roared out of the gates and down the road. She went back inside and dialled Dermot's number.

'Yes, please,' she said very quietly to his answering machine. 'I would like to visit your yacht.'

Over the next few days, Sue was busy organising help for the kennels. Michelle agreed to come and stay over the weekend, along with her best friend from school. The girls were reliable and Michelle's mother had promised to keep her eye on them. Much to Dermot's disgust, she insisted on taking William with her. She didn't want to leave any extra work for the two girls. Besides, if there was to be any sort of future with Dermot, he had to get used to William being around.

For Sue, the organisation occupied

only a very small part of her thoughts. Convincing herself that she wasn't making a grave error was the greatest task. She missed having Andy around, not that she could have spoken to him about her worries on this occasion.

Dermot collected her in his large, powerful car early on Saturday morning. William sat in the back, his tail wagging. They reached the mooring at noon and parked close to one of the larger yachts, to unload the car.

'Oh, Dermot, it's beautiful.'

She was quite awed by the size of the white craft with its perfect smooth line. She stepped on to the deck and held Will's lead tightly. She could see why Dermot had wanted to leave the dog behind. The boat was certainly not dog-friendly. She tied him to the rail while she helped unload everything. William's basket took its place on the deck and once commanded to sit and stay, he behaved impeccably.

Below deck there were two cabins. She would never have agreed to make the trip at all, unless the sleeping arrangements were sorted out satisfactorily, well in advance. She stood in her cabin and peered out of the porthole. The sea was a brilliant blue and she could hear the gentle slapping of rigging against masts, as the gentle breeze ruffled the shore.

She looked round. The double bunk was covered in a pretty floral duvet and fitted cupboards gave plenty of storage space. The light-coloured wood gave a remarkable feeling of spaciousness. It was so much grander than her own room at home. If she were to believe Dermot's declaration of love, this could all become a part of her everyday life. What a prospect, she thought. She rinsed her face, combed her hair and went up on deck. William greeted her as if she had been away for weeks.

'I hope he isn't going to be quite so wild when we set off,' Dermot said with doubt in his voice. 'I think there may be some kennels at the marina if you'd prefer to leave him.'

'Of course, I won't leave him. I'd have left him at home, if I'd had any doubts. He'll be fine, once he gets used to the motion of the boat.'

'OK. If you're sure, we'll get on our way. We'll anchor for lunch, once we're clear of the marina. There should be plenty of food in the fridge. You can take a look and see what you fancy.'

When he was satisfied that all was ready, he asked her to untie the stern and push them off.

'How will I get back on the boat?' she wailed.

'Haven't you ever been sailing? Untie it and jump back on. You push off with the boat hook.'

Sue frowned, feeling rather silly. She had never been on a boat, except during childhood trips to the local boating lake. He didn't have to make her feel quite so inept, especially in front of the crowds of people wandering round the quay. Was this whole thing a ghastly mistake, she wondered.

'Sorry, Sue,' Dermot said later when

they had stopped for lunch. 'I was being a pain. Forgive me?'

Sue smiled. How could she remain sulky on such a beautiful day in such wonderful surroundings? The kennels, her worries about her mother, all seemed miles away. She munched on a smoked salmon sandwich and sipped ice-cold white wine. After lunch, they sailed along the coast a short distance under power. Dermot asked if she'd like to try sailing. Game for anything by this time, she readily agreed.

The massive mainsail was hauled up and the engine stopped. There was a gentle breeze, enough to drive them along at a reasonable pace without being too energetic. The silence struck Sue. The sound of the water swishing by and the hum of the wind in the rigging seemed quite magical.

'I always love the idea of harnessing nature to give us motion,' Dermot said almost dreamily. 'I feel this is my real home, the only place I can be totally myself and totally at ease.'

Sue could only agree. Already, he looked younger. The worry lines she had noticed at times had disappeared.

'Right, we need to tack. When I call out ready-about, turn, grab that sheet and release it from the cleat. Then move to the other side and get the other as tight as you can. Ready?'

Sue had virtually no idea what he was talking about, but assumed the sheet was really a rope, as that was where he was pointing. As he yelled, Sue moved swiftly, scared of doing something wrong. When William heard the sharp command, he growled at Dermot and crouched as if waiting to pounce.

'Get the blasted dog under control,' he demanded. 'He looks as if he's about to flatten me. Get back, you stupid animal.'

The shouting was just too much for William. For the first time in his life, he actually attacked, growling ferociously, as he believed he was defending his beloved mistress.

'William, down,' Sue yelled, and he

obeyed, immediately looking at her with a very hurt expression. 'It's all right, boy. Now sit.'

'I told you to leave him behind. Now, for goodness' sake, get hold of those sheets.'

After this experience, Dermot decided that they might be better to use the engine and they motored along to a tiny cove, where the anchor was dropped on a long chain. He seemed to have forgiven and even forgotten the earlier incident. It was glorious, so peaceful and quite deserted. There was no access to the beach from the shore, so they had the place to themselves.

They dived into the water and Sue swam strongly to the shore. Not wanting to be left behind, William leaped into the water and swiftly paddled after her. He shook once they had landed then tore off among the rocks.

Dermot came to lie beside her on the beach and put his arm round her.

'I do love you, Sue,' he whispered. 'Say you love me.'

'You hardly know me. What little time we have spent together, you are usually criticising me or we argue about something, usually William. How can you love me? I'm not sure you even know what love means.'

'I've always had to fend for myself. It's become second nature to be bossy and boring. I promise you, give me a chance and I'll change. My parents both died when I was young and most of my younger life was spent in various boarding schools or staying at summer camps. I envy you the love of parents. Even your pesky dog loves you to death. Will you try, Sue? Try to love me, I mean, just a little?'

'Oh, Dermot, I'm so confused. You are everything anyone could want one minute and angry the next. I can't keep up. I'm sorry you had such a rotten childhood but you can't just turn love on like a switch. I do find you attractive but you can't buy me. However rich you are, it's the person that counts in the end. Take your time. Let's get to know each other properly.'

He leaned over and very gently kissed her lips.

'You taste all salty.' He laughed softly. 'OK. Agreed. I won't try to hurry things too much, as long as you give me a little hope.'

She smiled up at him and felt the world almost grind to a halt.

Dermot behaved like a perfect gentleman for the rest of the weekend. He rested an arm across her shoulders occasionally, kissed her a few times but made no more demands on her. He did, however, keep a wary eye on William whenever he was close to Sue. The dog seemed to have accepted the situation but was ever watchful in case he was needed!

All too soon, it was Monday morning and they were driving back to Nancetowan.

'It's been a wonderful weekend. I feel so relaxed,' Sue said. 'Thank you so much.'

‘My pleasure. It doesn’t have to be the end, you know. How about a trip to France next weekend? We can go by boat or even fly over, whatever you like. I have to go to the States the following week so it will be the last chance for a while. Unless you’d like to come with me. We could make it into a holiday. I have business in New York for a couple of days but I daresay you could find something to do while I have my meetings. What do you say?’

‘The States? Just like that? I have a business to run. I can’t take time off just like that. And there’s my mother. I can’t go away for days at a time. Who would visit her? She’d be dreadfully upset, and there’s William, too. I can’t abandon him.’

‘Easy sorted. You managed it this weekend. Why not again? I’m talking about our future here. You can’t seriously put your kennels before a future with me. I don’t think you realise how much money I have. I was in at the right time before computers started their boom. You'll never need to work again. Your mother can stay in the nursing home. She's happy there. I can pay for her to live in luxury for the rest of her life.'

'But I enjoy working. I love my job. OK, I get worried at times about making ends meet but it's a challenge. I thrive on it.'

'I don't understand you, Sue. It's that builder, isn't it? That's why you don't love me.'

'Don't be foolish. Andy is my friend. My best friend maybe, but still only a friend.'

'He's always round at your place, even at night. I've seen him there. Oh, Sue, why can't you see what you're turning down? I can be everything you want in a man. We can afford the very best of everything. I'll build a fur-lined kennel for William if that's what you want. You can have a dozen Williams. I can build a personal kennels for you to keep them all in, if it would make you happy. You can have someone just to look after them.'

'Please, Dermot, drive me home now. I'm just so confused. Thank you again for everything but I have to have time to think. You still don't seem to understand me. I can't be bought, not for money, possessions, foreign holidays or anything else.'

'Maybe that's what I love about you, what is so special about you. Every other woman I've ever known has a cash register sign lighting her eyes. You are real, warm and so very feminine. I do love you, but, I'll give you time to think. I just beg you, please don't leave me waiting for too long.'

Sue was relieved to find everything in good order when she returned to the kennels. The girls had managed well and seemed to have enjoyed themselves. They would come any time, they said, though she doubted their parents would be too pleased if she asked them again the following week! After lunch, Sue drove to see her mother. It was still lovely weather and Mrs Saunders was sitting outside in the lovely garden at the nursing home.

'Hello, dear. Fancy you coming again to see me. So very kind of you.'

'Hello, Mum. Sorry I wasn't here for the last couple of days. I had a little holiday.'

'Your young man came instead. He said he was leaving. I hope this doesn't mean you are going to get a divorce.'

Sue frowned. What on earth was her mother talking about now?

'I haven't got a young man, and I'm not married, so I can't get a divorce.'

'The gardener fellow, the one that does buildings. Can't remember his name. He came to say goodbye anyhow.'

'You must mean Andy,' Sue said softly.

Maybe he had really gone. He'd threatened to leave Cornwall when he was so cross about her going away with Dermot. She thought he had just been making a threat. When she finished her visit, she stopped off at Andy's mother's. Her reception did not have the usual warmth. In fact, Alice was quite off-hand with her.

11

I suppose you'd better come in,' Alice said grudgingly. 'I suppose you've heard?' she added as they went indoors.'

'What? What have I heard?' Sue asked, puzzled.

'He's gone. Andy's left. His father's furious. Left us both in the lurch. Graham was hoping to retire in a couple of years, and leave Andy to run the business. I simply don't know what's going to happen now. And how's Graham supposed to manage on his own? He has work lined up for the both of them for months ahead. How does it look if he has to let people down? We don't work like that, not in Cornwall.'

'I'm so sorry, Alice. I didn't know he really meant it. I just thought he was angry with me.'

'That's as maybe. You've broken his

heart, you know, and mine with it. I never thought I'd lose my only son, not like this. I was that pleased when he took up with a local girl. Well, one who's as good as local. Your aunt was highly thought of round here and we gave you credit for being the same. Shows how wrong you can be, doesn't it?'

'I'd better go,' Sue said.

She felt tears stabbing her eyes and knew that she had to get away from the accusations, however unjust.

'I'll see you soon,' she added out of pure habit.

'I don't think so. You are not welcome here any more. I'm sorry, but my husband's said so. Put his foot down. He's disappointed in you.'

Sue nodded. She understood how deeply loyalty was felt in this small community. She had lost her chances with the entire village, no doubt. So what? If she accepted Dermot's proposed future, she need never worry again about money, respect or anything else. She drove round the little village green and back to her own home.

What exactly had Dermot offered? He'd called it love. He'd offered everything money could buy. Had he actually offered marriage? She may be old-fashioned, but marriage came first in her book. Maybe she needed to ask him.

Mrs Bannister, the housekeeper, answered her ring at the door, as usual.

'I'll see if he's home,' she said in her businesslike manner.

'It's OK, I'm here Mrs B. Hello, darling. Have you come to tell me your decision?'

'It's scarcely a few hours since we parted. No, I haven't made up my mind yet. There are one or two more questions I need to ask.'

'Fire away,' he said as they sat down in his study.

'Do you intend to offer marriage?' she asked bluntly.

'Wow! You don't pull any punches. Isn't marriage rather final? I mean, well, you said it yourself. We hardly know each other. Surely we would need to know each other better before making the final big commitment. Or are you saying you will only consider marriage and nothing else?'

'I think I have my answers from what you say.'

'But I've only asked you questions.'

'That told me what I wanted to hear.'

'Sue, I'll marry you of course, if that's what you want, right away. There, I've never said that to a living soul before.'

He looked pleased with himself and Sue smiled.

'I still think I need more time. I'll have to go now. I must see to the dogs and get back to my work properly. I haven't done a thing today. Not really.'

'You'll never have to work again, remember, if we're married. And,' he added as a flurry of barking sounded from next door, 'we won't have to live next to a noisy kennels.'

Sue glared at him. If she'd had

doubts before, suddenly they were all gone. She could neither live with nor marry this man. She would never be her own person again. She would never have her independence. She would be at his beck and call, night and day. No, however attractive the life sounded, without her own interests and her beloved dogs, she would cease to be Sue Saunders.

'I won't keep you in suspense any longer, Dermot. I realise I don't love you at all. I could never marry you. I'm happy to be friends but I won't be any more than that.'

'But why? Couldn't you even learn to love me, just a little?'

He looked so woe-begone that she almost laughed.

'You're a lovely man and have everything going for you. But it doesn't include marriage to me. Everything is wrong. You'll find the right woman one day, I'm sure. Thank you for asking me. I'm very flattered, as I said before.'

'Oh, Sue, if you ever change your mind . . . '

She shook her head.

'It's Andy, isn't it?'

'Maybe, but he's left Cornwall. I've blown my chances with him.'

Feeling suddenly sad, she turned and left Dermot standing in his beautiful house, filled with his treasures. Poor little rich boy, she thought.

On some sort of auto-pilot, she did the evening chores. She took some of the larger dogs out to play in the field for a while. She wouldn't have it for much longer so she needed to make the most of it. She went into each of the dogs in her care and petted them. William stood outside each door, waiting for her to come out. He greeted her with such enthusiasm, she had to smile.

'You're my best friend, aren't you, boy? Always there for me.'

Truly unconditional love, she thought. Certainly not what Dermot could offer but that wasn't really his fault. He had never had the same opportunity as she'd had, nor Andy, come to think of it. Andy . . . he always offered unconditional love. He was good-hearted, generous and fun to be with. He was a hard worker and might never have the sort of wealth Dermot could offer, but he had the true capacity for loving another person.

'I miss him, Wills,' she whispered into the soft fur.

She had left it too late. She realised too late that it had been Andy all the time. She had been so busy thinking of herself and her precious kennels, that she had not given enough time to this generous man. She had even thought of him as a sort of brother. How stupid was she? He was the man for her. She really needed him. The thought of never seeing him again was almost more than she could bear. She called to her dog.

'Come on, boy, let's get some supper.'

Over the next few days, she tried

every way she knew to try and find out where Andy had gone. She approached the surfing crowd but they could tell her nothing. She visited the local pubs to see if anyone had heard him mention his plans. She even visited Alice again, braving the woman's disapproval in her attempts to locate Andy, but he had disappeared totally.

'Serves me right,' she told William angrily. 'I took him for granted and now I've lost him.'

William whined. He didn't understand why she was angry with him. She smiled.

'Sorry, boy. It isn't you. Come on. Let's go for a run.'

They went to the beach. It was the end of September and the dog ban was over. The dog cavorted through the waves, barking madly and chasing the odd gulls when they dared swoop anywhere near him. Sue watched. This was where she wanted to be. How could she be lonely in a place like this? With William and all the other dogs to keep her company, it wasn't a bad life. Somehow, she would find enough money to keep her mother at the nursing home where she had settled and seemed quite content. It wouldn't be easy but she would manage somehow.

She whistled William and walked to the end of the beach. It was beginning to get dark. Suddenly, William stopped, gave a short bark and hurled himself at the rocks. A frantic barking broke out, together with the short yaps he always made when he was excited. Sue ran over. William was leaping all over a man who had been sitting quietly among the rocks.

'Hello, Sue,' Andy said, getting to his feet.

'Andy!' she yelled. 'What on earth are you doing here? We all thought you'd gone away.'

She flung herself at him, holding him in a tight hug.

'Gosh, we've missed you.'

'Have you really?' he asked doubtfully. 'I thought it was all on for you, with that Dermot fellow.'

'I made a mistake. I only thought I was attracted to him.'

Andy stared at her. She stood on tiptoe and reached up to kiss the man she now knew for certain she loved. She put her arms up and pulled him towards her. He bent to reach her soft mouth and kissed her tenderly. There was no hint of the brotherly pecks she had experienced before. This time, everything was real. She had discovered the elusive magic she had been seeking for so long, and it had been waiting here for her, all the time.

'Come on, Sue. Let's go and tell Mum we're both well and truly home.'

'What a lot of time we have wasted.'

'Promise we won't waste any more?'

'Woof, woof!' William barked, having the last word as usual.

'We'll soon make up for it, don't you worry,' Sue said happily.